T0209206

MY STREET, MY FRIENDS

E. Davis-Banks

authorHOUSE®

AuthorHouse™
1663 Liberty Drive
Bloomington, IN 47403
www.authorhouse.com
Phone: 1 (800) 839-8640

Published by AuthorHouse 08/30/2016

ISBN: 978-1-5246-2182-7 (sc)
ISBN: 978-1-5246-2183-4 (hc)
ISBN: 978-1-5246-2181-0 (e)

Library of Congress Control Number: 2016912413

Print information available on the last page.

Chapter 1

The street is layered in orange, yellow, and brown leaves that continuously flutter down. It's warm in the early afternoon. The wide street is lined with old, large, and beautiful homes with porches and patios out front decorated with mums, and some have swings. Many trees form a canopy. It looks like a picture you'd see on a postcard. Birds are flying around, and squirrels are busy searching for nuts to store for the winter. All is quiet.

A humming sound gets louder, closer. The birds fly away. The squirrels run up trees. Four heads pop up over the hill in the street. Children of about ten and eleven are laughing as they race each other on loud, motorized scooters. Two jump off their scooters with legs in the air and hands on the handles. One child, not that experienced on the scooter, is riding very carefully. Another's head is bobbing to the music he's listening to on his iPod.

Lance, Helen, Robert, and Dee are coming home from the community center, where they go every Saturday. School has been in session for a week, and they're having fun on the weekend. They all go home; Lance and Dee are the last ones to do so.

"Lance, why are you so quiet?" Dee asks.

Lance shrugs his shoulders and keeps going. He thinks to himself, *I wish she would just leave me alone!* He speeds up so he is in front of her.

Dee speeds up too. "You can't beat me!"

Lance speeds up, but Dee shoots by him. Lance is laughing, not paying attention to the street. A car appears. Dee yells, "Lance!" so loud the other children who are about to go into their homes stop and look down the street.

Robert runs to Lance. By the time he gets there, Lance has swerved to the right and hit a garbage can in a driveway. Garbage flies everywhere; some lands on Lance, who ends up covered in it. His friends are laughing so hard they have to hold their stomachs as Lance just sits, a little dizzy. His father, who was driving the car, jumps out and runs to him.

His friends are asking, "Lance? You all right?" Robert is laughing and Helen is giggling.

Lance's father is panicked. He picks him up. "Are you okay?"

"I—I'm okay, I think. Is the car okay?"

"Never mind the car, young man. Get your stuff and get in the house now!"

Lance hangs his head, picks up his stuff, and heads into the house. Lance's father yells, "Go get the broom and start cleaning this mess up now!"

I wish my dad wasn't so serious. We never have any fun. He's always working, Lance thinks as he looks at his father's scooter in the garage just collecting dust. He'd bought two scooters so he and Lance could spend quality time together, but Lance's father has used his only once. He places his scooter next to his dad's. He shakes his head. As he enters the kitchen, he can smell the food his mother is cooking.

"The same thing again?" he asks. His guess is correct. His mother is a good cook but repeatedly cooks the same thing. *I'm going to be a chef one day and make different meals every day.* He wishes his mother would get another cookbook.

His mother sees him and gives him a hug. "What's wrong?"

He tells his mother the whole story. She checks his arms and legs, head, stomach. Lance is squirming. She asks, "You okay?"

"Yes, Mom, I'm okay. Stop kissing on me! I have to get the broom and help Dad clean up the mess outside. He's really mad!"

By the time Lance gets to the driveway with a broom, he sees that his father has already picked up most of the garbage. Lance begins to sweep up the rest, wondering what his father is thinking. Both are silent. Lance's father gets into his car and drives it into the garage. He gets out, looks at his son from head to toe, and goes in.

Robert sees Lance on the street with his father looking down at him. He chuckles and shakes his head as he pushes his scooter into his garage. He loves rap music and wants to be a famous rapper someday. He's always listening to rap on his iPod, which he's proud of. He'd raked leaves, watered and mowed lawns during the spring and summer, and shoveled snow for his older neighbors in the winter. He saved his money; his parents were surprised when they saw how much he had saved. He asked his parents to take him to the electronics store to buy the iPod. His father had felt he was too young to have one, but he let him get it since he had worked so hard for it. He'd been proud of his son for all the good grades he'd earned in school and for having made the honor roll.

Robert enters the kitchen. His sister, Bobbie, is doing homework at the kitchen table. He playfully pulls one of her braids and runs up to his room. Bobbie immediately takes off after him. Their mother comes into the kitchen to check her dinner.

"You all better stop all that running in this house! Get started on your chores if you don't have homework."

"I have homework," Bobbie yells. "Robert was pulling my hair!"

"Robert, stop messing with your sister! She has work to do."

Bobbie sticks her tongue out at her brother and runs downstairs to her homework. Robert just smiles and goes to his room. He looks into his backpack to get his homework. He looks out the window while lying in bed. A cardinal flies to his window ledge and tries to look in. *It's good luck to see a red cardinal!*

The bird keeps trying to see in. Robert just lets it be and starts his homework. Education is very important in Robert's house. "All our children are going to be something," their mother always said. Robert's dad is a construction worker and makes pretty good money, and Robert's mother works as a school cook. Robert likes that because he always gets goodies she brings from his school. Today, his mother brought home brownies. He likes his mother even though she's tough when it comes to chores and homework. She always gives them hugs and tells them she loves them. He'll have some brownies after he finishes his homework. He has math to do and some literature also. He loves literature. It's full of adventures. Whether it's make-believe or factual, he likes to read period.

But Robert really loves rap, all kinds. He memorizes the rap and tries his best to talk as fast as the rappers. He considers himself a pro but knows deep down he has a lot of work to do. His mother hates rap. She doesn't like how they use curse words or talk about women, so she constantly monitors what he listens to. One day, she heard Robert curse while listening to his iPod; Robert hadn't realized she was right behind him.

She had yanked his earphones off. "I told you about cursing in this house!" She took his iPod away for a week. And boy, did he have to do a lot of chores that week. He didn't realize how technical his mother was. She managed to erase all the music with curse words in it. Robert was sure his older brother had helped her.

He knows his mother and father are good parents. Sometimes when he listens to his music, it does sound bad. He doesn't like everything he hears and wonders why black people always sound so mad. He thinks his race is always mad about something but doesn't know why.

Robert is almost finished with his homework when his older brother, William, comes into the room. "Robert, get your buns downstairs. Dinner's ready."

"Okay, I'm coming down. How was football practice?"

"It was okay. I'm doing pretty well, bro!"

They go downstairs. Robert likes his big brother.

Helen was outside watering the garden while waiting for dinner. When her mother got home, she ran in to tell her what had happened to Lance. Her mother was very concerned that Lance had been hurt, but when she found out he wasn't, she laughed loudly. "Helen, you made my day. I needed something to laugh out today."

Helen knew her mother had been sad. Her father was in Iraq fighting in the war. Helen hated the war. Her father was a good man and didn't need to be killing people. They loved being a family. He loved to water the grass and take care of the yard and garden, which was beautiful—full of pink and orange tulips and sunflowers that were still blooming.

She and her dad used to have good talks in the garden; her father always made her laugh. She was scared he wouldn't laugh when he came back though he always told her he would. She never understood war. Her father told her that it was his responsibility to help bring peace to the world and that there were bad men who didn't want peace. He told her it was the world's responsibility to make sure the bad guys didn't have too much power because they wouldn't treat people fairly. She was glad her father was a good man; she missed him. He had one more year to serve.

Her mother was sad sometimes, and it was hard for her to cheer her mother up. She was glad she could tell a funny story about Lance. Just as Helen was finishing up the watering, her mother yelled through the kitchen window, "Helen, dinner's ready!"

Helen was hungry. "What's for dinner, Momma?"

"Fried chicken, macaroni and cheese, salad, and apple pie for dessert."

"Sounds good!"

Helen loved her mother's cooking, and she loved to hear her sing while she worked. Her mother said singing and cooking were her favorite things.

After dinner, they'd always go to their family computer in the living room and email her father; they enjoyed that. Sometimes, they wouldn't hear from him for weeks, but other times, they heard from him right away. He was in a very dangerous area and had to be careful.

That evening, he responded right away. He always asked her about her homework and how school was going. Helen was quickly learning how to type. While her mother was at the computer, the phone rang. "Helen, please answer that."

She did. It was Dee's mother.

"Hello, Helen. How are you? Is your mother around?"

"Yes she is, but she's on the computer with my dad right now."

Dee's mother sounded worried. "Could you ask her to call me at work when she's done?" Helen said yes and hung up just as her mother got off the computer.

"Your dad is happy. It looks like he might be coming home for a break in three months!"

Helen was excited to hear that great news and could see her mother was as well.

"Who called?"

"Dee's mother. She wanted you to call her at work."

Helen's mother called her back. After she hung up, she said, "Helen, get your jacket on. We're going to get Dee and have her spend the night. Her mother has to work late and her grandmother is out of town this week."

Helen was excited about having company. "All right, Momma. Can she sleep with me tonight?"

"I don't think so. It's a school night, and you all talk all night long when you're together. You two can watch a movie and then it's bedtime. I'll let her sleep in the guest room."

As they walked to Dee's, Helen watched squirrels gathering nuts and admired the colorful leaves. She liked that time of year. She knew winter would arrive soon, and she loved Christmas. "What about their cat? Can we bring her also?" Helen asked.

"No, but we'll make sure she has enough food and water. She'll be all right."

"Dee told me she doesn't know where her father is. She told me her father and mother were divorced. It must be hard for her because all her friends have fathers."

"Yes, you're right. It must be hard. You know it's hard for us because your father's in Iraq, but that's why she has good neighbors like us. We can take care of her when her mother needs us."

Helen smiled and held her mother's hand, something she'd been doing for as long as she could remember. Her mother always said, "When you're out with me, you hold my hand. That way, strangers know I'm protecting you and I know where you are." Helen sometimes thought she was too old to hold hands, but she felt good and safe when she did.

When they got to Dee's door, she was looking out the window and waving. She opened the door. "Hello, Mrs. Smith. Hi, Helen. I got my clothes for tomorrow already packed and my pajamas too. Do I need anything else?"

"Your toothbrush," Helen's mom said. "I have everything else you might need. Is the cat's food okay?"

"Yep! Momma told me to fill her bowl with food and give her some fresh water. She's sleeping on her bed. Here's the extra door key Momma told me to give you."

"You two wait on the front porch," Helen's mother said. "I'll make sure the backdoor is secure and set the alarm."

Helen and Dee were excited about Dee's spending the night. They'd been good friends ever since they could remember. Their mothers were also good friends.

"What are we going to do tonight? You think your mother will let us call Robert and Lance?"

Helen laughed. "You might as well get that out of your head right now. My mother will not let us call boys!"

"But they're our friends, not just some old boys!"

"Momma already told me we can watch a movie. She'll pop some popcorn. Did you do all your homework?"

"Yeah," Dee said, "and I have my books for school tomorrow."

"I guess that will have to do."

They laughed. By that time, Helen's mother was locking the front door. They walked down the block to Helen's home and went in. Helen's mother showed her where she was going to sleep. Helen asked again if she could sleep with her, and her mother again said no. Dee frowned, but she liked the guest room bed better than Helen's because it was so soft and fluffy.

Helen's mom asked them if they had finished their homework, and both nodded. "Then pick out a movie from Helen's movie shelf."

They ran to the den and started to search for a movie they both liked while Helen's mother started preparing the popcorn. She also made some Kool-Aid. *This will keep them both busy while I work on my sewing,* she thought.

It was a good evening for all on that street. By 9:00 p.m., the four friends were sleeping peacefully.

Chapter 2

On Monday morning, Lance's alarm went off. He looked at the clock with one eye. He didn't want to get up. He didn't want to go to school. *Why don't we have three-day weekends? That would give me more hours to rest and play.*

"Lance! Get up now!" his father yelled.

"I'm up, Dad!" He got up and rubbed his eyes. He looked in his pet gerbil's cage and said good morning. The gerbil looked at him and wiggled its nose. It was his fifth gerbil; the others had gone to gerbil heaven. He liked having gerbils but felt they didn't live all that long. It was sad when he lost them, but for some reason, he had to have one in his room. They cheered him up, and he could train them to not run away when they were out of the cage. This gerbil was the best one yet. He could let him out during homework, and the gerbil would sit next to his book and sleep! It was the funniest thing.

Lance took a shower. By the time he was dressed, his mother yelled, "Breakfast is ready! Hurry up!" Lance ran downstairs and sat at the kitchen table. His father was drinking coffee and reading the paper. He was always reading the newspaper morning, noon, and night. Lance thought that one day his father would turn into a newspaper or his nose would get stuck in the pages. Lance giggled at his thoughts.

His father looked over his paper. "What's so funny?"

"Oh, nothing. Mom, what's for breakfast?"

"Bacon, scrambled eggs, and pancakes. Do you think that's enough for you this morning?"

"Yeah! Hand them over!"

Lance quickly ate and ran to get his books. He had to walk to school and wanted to meet his friends; they always walked together. His mother gave him a kiss on his forehead. "Aww, Mom, that's baby stuff," he said as he squirmed while his mother hugged him. "You'll always be my baby, young man. Now get to school."

Lance ran out the door and right back in to say good-bye to his father. His father said, "Was wondering if I'd get a good-bye today." He smiled at his son. Lance raced back out the door.

Robert's morning hadn't been as good as Lance's. He got up late and had to rush. He had a bowl of cold cereal because his mother had to go to work early and his father couldn't cook well at all. Robert's brother could cook, but he had to go to football practice before classes started. Robert's little sister was just getting up. Everybody was rushing around the house like worker ants. Robert had to wait for his little sister to get out of the bathroom. They had two bathrooms, but with all of them in the home, at times, it was hard with all of them trying to get ready for school and work. This really frustrated Robert. *When I grow up, I'm going to be rich and have bathrooms in every bedroom.*

He went downstairs to iron his jeans. He always ironed his clothes; he was a very neat person. He put on his earphones and started listening to rap while he ironed. Afterward, he poured cereal into his bowl, went to the refrigerator to get milk, and ate, his head bobbing the whole time.

His sister came from upstairs and told him she was finished with the bathroom. He hurriedly ran upstairs before anyone could beat him to the bathroom. The shower was nice and hot. It was lukewarm sometimes, but not that day. He took a quick shower, brushed his teeth and combed his hair in just five minutes, and dressed in three. He ran downstairs and got his backpack and iPod. His mother, sister, and father were all running around trying to get ready to go. He was the first to go in the morning. "See y'all later!" he yelled. Everyone responded, "See you later!"

He was off to meet the other kids. He liked walking to school. He could listen to his iPod. His other friends knew he wouldn't talk much, but sometimes, he'd turn it off to talk with them. He thought this would be a good day for him to talk, so when he got to the corner, he would turn it off.

Helen's alarm went off about 6:30 a.m. She liked to wake up early and take a long shower. Today, she woke up earlier because Dee was there. They had only one shower in the house, and she wanted to be the first because sometimes it would be cold water instead of warm. She got up and headed for the bathroom. She could smell sausage and pancakes. *I'm going to have a good breakfast!*

Her mother always cooked a good breakfast; she always said you got a good start to your day by eating a good meal. Her mother was a housewife when her dad was home, but she'd gotten a part-time job to make ends meet; she was a seamstress at a wedding boutique and liked her work. She told Helen, "I like jobs where people always come in happy." She worked from nine until noon three days a week, so she was always home when Helen came in from school. She thought she had the greatest parents ever.

Dee woke about twenty minutes later. She'd forgotten she wasn't in her bed. She had slept so well after a fun evening. They'd watched a great movie, and the popcorn was good. She sat up in bed and thought how nice her friends were. She thought she would always have Helen for a friend. She wondered if her cat missed her but thought she was okay and her mother would be home soon.

By the time she got up, Helen was done with her shower, so she went to take hers. Helen stated, "Dee, hurry up! Momma's cooked pancakes and sausage!"

"You know I like her pancakes," Dee said. "I'll be right down!"

After breakfast, they grabbed their backpacks and scurried downstairs, where Helen's mother was waiting for them. She gave them lunch money and rushed them out the door. "Have a good day at school!"

They both waved at her. Dee said to Helen," I'm glad we're close friends. Your mother and mine are like sisters."

"I'm glad too," Helen said. "I wish you could spend the night every night."

"I think my mother would miss me and so would my kitty. Hey! Maybe you could spend the night with me tonight!"

"My mother won't let me on school nights unless it's an emergency like yours," Helen said. "I'll ask her if I can Friday night. Isn't you mother off work?"

"Yes, and she doesn't have any plans so far. I'll ask her if it's okay."

They ran down to the corner to meet the boys, something the four of them had been doing since kindergarten. The school was just two blocks away. Their neighborhood was pretty good—no bullies. There used to be one on the block. He'd tried to pick a fight with Lance one day, and Robert came up and dared him to hit him instead. The bully looked at Robert and ran. Shortly after that, the bully's family moved, and that was the end of that. Their street was calm, peaceful. It was a good street, and everybody knew each other. All the adults looked after each other and their homes especially if they were on vacation.

All was quiet on the street. They heard birds chirping and saw squirrels scampering around. A few of the older neighbors were tending their gardens. It was a good street.

Chapter 3

It was the end of the day. Helen went to her locker to get her backpack. She didn't like carrying it around during the day, so she carried her books. When she got to her locker, Lance was waiting for her.

"Hey Helen, what's up?"

"Hey Lance! How were classes today?"

"It was funny today. Harry Petersen put tacks on Old Mr. Pont's chair!"

"What! Did he get in trouble?"

Lance laughed. "No. You know Mr. Pont. He's so mean he doesn't let anyone know if he's hurting. He sat down on the tacks and made this funny face. Most of the class kept a straight face. Harry tried real hard not to laugh but kept giggling, and loud too. But guess what? Mr. Pont went out of the room with all those tacks in his behind. I wanted to fall down laughing. But you know, it wasn't worth it. After he came back, he gave us all extra homework and said that he was calling all our parents to tell them what had happened and that he expected all of us to have the work done or he'd give us an F!"

Helen laughed.

"What's so funny? I'm going to be working on this all night! And I didn't do anything."

"This is happening because no one would tell, right?"

"I'm no snitch," said Lance, who still smiled about it. "Don't you think that man looks like a vampire?"

They laughed.

"Let's wait for the others. I did all my homework in class today. I don't have to do anything when I get home," said Helen.

"Don't rub it in," said Lance. "History is my worst subject. I could use your help."

"I'll ask my mother if I can come over, but you know a parent must be around."

"My mother will be home at four. I'll have her call your mom. See you then."

When Lance got home, his mother had already received a call from his history teacher. "Lance, I'm hoping you didn't have anything to do with this situation, did you?"

Lance smiled. "I wasn't smart enough to think of it."

His mother chuckled just a bit. "Well, young man, it looks like you'll be in the house anyway. He told me he'd give Fs to those who didn't do all the homework."

Lance frowned. "Mom, Helen wanted to come over and help me with the homework. You know how bad I am with history. Is it all right if she comes? We could work in the family room."

His mother nodded. He was going to call Helen to tell her it was okay for her to come and study with him. Lance had a secret crush on Helen anyway. He liked being around her and liked to talk to her. She was cool. She didn't think he was a nerd as Dee had called him once. Dee was okay, but she always made fun of him and thought he was square. Helen was different; she didn't judge people on how they looked. And her mother made good snacks. He liked Helen's dad too. It was a shame he was in Iraq. Lance couldn't imagine what it would be like to have a father or mother fighting in the war. His father had flat feet and couldn't serve in the armed services. He was very patriotic though and had the American flag on a pole in his yard.

Lance dialed Helen's number; it rang three times before she answered. "What took you so long?" he asked.

"I had to use the restroom. My mother said it was okay to come over for an hour, so we better study fast. I'm coming right over."

"Okay. I'll have everything set up. My mother is getting potato chips and pop ready for us. See you then. Hey, Helen, thanks again for helping me."

"No problem. You can help me in math some time. I'm not worried about it."

Lance got off the phone and was just about to go downstairs when the phone rang. It was Robert. "Hey man, can you come outside? I got a new football I want to break in."

"No, man. Our whole class got in trouble in history class today, and we got extra homework. Helen's coming over to help me."

"Whoa, dude! You're in that class? Everybody heard what happened. It's all over school. I think it's nice you're all sticking up for each other. I wish I was a little mouse so I could have seen the face on that teacher when he sat down on those tacks," he said with a laugh.

"Yeah, dude, but we're paying for it now. We all agreed no more tricks in class. Gotta go. Helen will be over any minute now. Sorry, maybe tomorrow."

Robert hung up and went downstairs to his brother's room. He was doing homework, "Hey, you wanna play catch?"

His brother looked up from his studying. "No. I got this big paper to do, and it's due in two days. I can play on the weekend."

Robert didn't like that answer, but what else could he do? There was no one to play with. His father had to work overtime, which he was always doing. Robert really liked his father and wanted to spend more time with him. His father had played football and basketball in college. His father was real tall. He remembered seeing his father's pictures in the old college newspaper. He played defensive back and was very good at it. His father was a lawyer and was good at that too. But he wished he could spend more time with his dad. *Oh well. Maybe I'll see if anyone needs their lawn raked.* He got his rake and told his mother he was going to work for some money.

His mother, who was always worried about him going to other people's homes, said, "Make sure you watch out and only go to those homes where you've done chores before."

Robert nodded his head and went on his way. He loved raking for the older neighbors; some of them would give him treats and extra money if he did a good job. He considered some of them cheap because they didn't pay him enough, but in any case, he always did a good job.

As he was walking, Dee came out of her home and called out to him. "Robert, what are you getting ready to do?"

Robert saw her coming. *Oh Lord. I wanted to be left alone, but here comes Dee.* Robert thought she was a good friend, but once in a while, she was a pest. It was one of those days that he wanted to be with his brother or father, not a girl.

On the other hand, Dee loved to be with Robert, whom she considered a cool kid. She had a little crush on him. "Can I come with?"

He looked at her. For some reason, he couldn't say no to her. "Yeah, you can come along, but don't you bug me today with those dry jokes."

"What do you mean dry jokes? I tell the best jokes in town! I mean, you laugh at all of them. I can help you bag leaves, and you can give me a dollar," she said with a smile.

He laughed. "Who said I'm going to give you a dollar?"

The day was almost over. The sun was going down. Robert saw Old Man Davis on his porch and said to Dee, "Old Man Davis looks lazy today, and maybe he'll want us to clean his lawn."

Old Man Davis saw him coming. He thought of going inside before the kids got there, but he hesitated. *I can't do that to those kids. They're trying to earn some money, and Lord knows I don't want to rake my lawn. But I wonder how much they're going to charge me. I won't pay them more than seven bucks.*

Robert came up to the porch. "Good evening, sir. Would you like to have your lawn raked?"

Old Man Davis looked at the two. "How much?"

"How about six dollars?" asked Robert.

Old Man Davis looked at them. "I'll give you no more than ten," he said with a smile. "Do you think you can do both front and back before dark?"

Robert and Dee nodded.

"Well get to work then!"

Robert and Dee got right to work. It was nice to know their neighbors were willing to pay them for their work.

"Hey, now you can give me two dollars!" Dee said.

Robert smiled. "Okay, you can have two dollars, no more. I'm trying to save up."

They raked and raked but stopped from time to time to jump into the leaves; they'd laugh at whoever made the bigger mess. Robert and Dee were good friends, and it was fun playing together. Robert hoped they'd be friends forever.

Chapter 4

A couple of days had passed. It was Friday. School had just let out. Robert and Lance were walking out of the school together as they normally did.

"Boy, am I glad this week is over. And guess what? I passed the extra homework that old teacher gave us for putting tacks on his seat," Lance said.

"Hey, who put those tacks on the seat anyway? Did you do that?"

"No way!" Lance said. "I'm too chicken. I'm not going to tell. Our class made a promise not to ever tell so the culprit wouldn't get suspended."

Robert nodded. "Yeah, I know. Anyway, I can't wait until we get home."

"Scooter time!" Lance said.

Robert and Lance gave each other high-fives.

"My dad gave me some fuel for my scooter, but he told me to earn some more money because gas was costing too much. Dee and I raked the lawn for Old Man Davis the other day, and he paid us ten bucks!"

"Ten dollars each?" Lance asked.

"No, silly. Ten bucks total. I gave Dee two for helping me."

"I wish you'd asked me to help you," Lance said. "I need the money."

"You were too busy doing that special homework project," he said with a laugh. "Anyway, your daddy doesn't want you to work. You all make so much money that you don't have to. And don't you have an allowance?"

"Not now. Dad took it away when I ran into the garbage can and nicked his bumper."

"Whoa, man, I didn't know you scratched your dad's car!" Robert said. "How long before you get off punishment?"

"I'm not on punishment. I can still ride the scooter. I just have to find my own gas money and give it to Dad so he can gas it up. I have twenty saved up, and I'm glad I didn't spend it. I spent only five on gas. I won't be able to ride as much as I'd like to. I can only go to the community center tomorrow."

"Not today?" Robert asked.

Lance shook his head. "I have some chores today."

Robert laughed. "Then you are on punishment."

"Let's run the rest of the way home. Bet I can beat you!" said Lance.

Lance was an excellent runner. He ran track and field for the community center and was considered a star. He had quite a few first-place ribbons. His father told him that someday they would be very important particularly when he got to high school and needed to prove to the coaches he was a good runner.

Robert could also run fast, and he liked the long jump. He had a few ribbons but not as many as Lance.

They lined up at a crack in the sidewalk. They glanced at each other. "On your mark, get set, go!" yelled Robert.

They took off. Lance was the better runner; he was ahead of Robert in seconds. The sidewalk was too narrow for them to run side by side, so Robert would jump over the hedges that lined some of the lawns. They were laughing as they raced. They passed many neighbors who would just wave and shake their heads.

Old Man Davis was on his porch. *Look at those kids running. Wish it were me.* He was seventy and too old to do much, he thought. He liked having children on the street, unlike some of the other older folks. His mother had told him years ago that children kept you young, that when children were around, the world was a brighter place. He agreed. Watching the kids was hilarious.

Lance and Robert were almost home. Robert's home was coming up first. Lance was definitely winning. He won by a mile. When they got to Robert's house, they fell in the yard, panting.

Robert's mother drove up just then. "Hey you two! How was your day?"

"It was a good day, Momma," Robert said. "Hey, any juice left? Can we have some?"

Robert's mother smiled. "Yes. Lance, go in and call your mother and ask her if it's okay for you to stay a while."

Lance and Robert ran into the house. Lance liked Robert's mother. Not only was she pretty, but she was very nice too. Lance remembered when Robert and his family first moved into the neighborhood. Lance's father was very concerned because they were a black family. Lance didn't understand why his father was so worried. His father thought they wouldn't take care of the house. Robert's parents had a better yard than they had. It was funny to see how grown-ups acted sometimes. Lance and Robert had been friends ever since Robert moved in, and Lance's father became friends with Robert's family. Lance's father said to his mother one day, "You know, I judged that family, and I was wrong. They're real nice people, and Lance feels safe there."

Lance agreed. He felt safe at Robert's home, and they always had good food there too. Not that Lance's mother couldn't cook, because she could, but Robert's mother made such good cookies and cake. Lance asked Robert's mother, "Excuse me, but do you have any more of those chocolate chip cookies?"

"Yes, look in the cookie jar, but wash your hand first."

They went to the bathroom after Lance called home to see if he could stay a while. Robert's mother asked them if they were going to the community center. Lance told her he was on punishment. Robert said he wanted to wait until tomorrow because a good movie was coming on TV that night. Lance asked Robert's mother if he could stay over and see the movie with Robert.

"Call your mother first and I'll talk to her. Do you have chores tonight?"

Lance hung his head. "Yes, I have to do a few things for my dad."

"Get home and do them quick. The movie doesn't start until seven. I'll call your mother and see if she'd like to come over and visit with me. Then she can walk you down because I don't want you walking by yourself in the dark."

"Okay," said Lance. "Thanks for calling my mom. See you later!" Lance ran home. *I'm going to get my chores done. It's going to be fun to see this movie with Robert. I hope it's sci-fi.*

When he got home, his mother was already talking to Robert's mother. They talked a while. Lance got the rake and yelled, "Mom, I'm going to rake the backyard."

"Good! Your dad wants it done before you do anything else."

Lance began raking. He thought he maybe shouldn't had raced Lance because he was tired, but he wanted to get back to Robert's house. He also liked Robert's brother, a football player who let Lance watch him work out on his equipment in the basement. The young boys weren't allowed to work out on the equipment; only Robert's father and older brother could, but it was fun to dream about one day being tall enough to do it. It looked fun to Lance, who wanted to be buff someday. Robert's father had told him he had a long way to go, but Lance smiled at that. He began to rake with all his might. The last time he went to visit Robert, they had ordered pizza because Robert's mother was too tired to cook. He was hoping she'd do that again.

It was almost dark. The leaves were colorful in the dim light. By the time Lance's mother came out to check on him, the yard was done.

"My, my! You've done quite an excellent job! Go in and shower. We have thirty minutes before the movie begins. And guess what? Robert's mother is ordering pizza! You all will watch one movie, and Robert's mother and I will watch another one in the living room."

Lance was very excited. He ran upstairs to shower *Perfect Friday! I'm so glad there's no school tomorrow.*

It was about six, and Helen had just finished cleaning her backyard. The wind was very blustery, and the night before, some tree branches has blown from the neighbor's yard into theirs. She knew her father always kept the yard up, and she was dead set on continuing that responsibility until her father got home from Iraq. Her mother was on the phone with her best friend, who lived about five miles away. She was worried about her mother. Not having her father around was hard on her. Sometimes, her mother would cry and stay in her bedroom away from her, and that was hard too. But lately, since she'd heard he was coming home early, she was in better spirits. That day was one of those days.

Helen took the rake and garbage bag full of branches to the garage. After putting everything where it was supposed to be, she cleaned her scooter and made sure it had enough fuel. When it was low, she'd let her mother know so they could buy more. The community center rules were that only the parents or another adult could gas up a scooter. Helen checked everything out; the scooter was good to go.

She loved riding her scooter. She'd just started riding it, but she was getting better each time she rode it. She'd begged her father to let her have a scooter, and he had given in against his better judgment. "I don't think a girl so be going around riding these things," he had said. Her mother stepped. "Yet during World War II, women built planes and test-flew them to make sure they were safe for soldiers like you to fly them!"

With that, her father had just hung his head. "Your mother's right. Women did do those great things for their men. I'm just concerned about you safety, that's all."

"Dad," Helen had said, "I'll make sure I follow all the safety rules, I promise. The moment I break the rules, you can take the scooter away."

Her father had looked lovingly into her eyes. *She's just like me—so adventurous, wanting to try anything and everything.* "Okay. Let's go looking for one tomorrow."

Helen remembered just how happy she was to know that her father trusted what she told him. She knew she had to follow the rules or her dad would take it away in a heartbeat.

She really missed talking to her dad. It was hard to know he was in Iraq. She saw the news every day and was scared her father would get hurt. But so far, he was okay and still emailing them. Every day, they would communicate with each other, so for the time being, that was okay.

"Helen, Dee's on the phone," her mother called out.

"Coming!" yelled Helen. She ran inside. It was almost time for her favorite TV show. She hoped Dee wouldn't talk long. She picked up the phone. "I got it Mom!" she yelled.

"Okay," responded her mother, who hung up and started to cook hamburgers for dinner.

"Hi, Dee. What's up?"

"Hey, Helen, I was calling to see if you had any fuel for my scooter."

"Don't you know your mother or another adult has to put it in?"

"Oh come on!" Dee yelled. "I put it in all the time. My mother doesn't know how."

"Do you have enough to get to the community center?"

"I think so. It's just below the refuel line. Do you think Mr. Smith will give me some more fuel tomorrow?" Dee asked.

"He always has a reserve tank on hand," said Helen. "I bet he can help you out when you get there. I don't have enough. My mother put the last of what I had in my scooter tank just a while ago."

"Okay," said Dee. "What are you doing tonight? Can you come over and spend the night?"

"No way, not tonight. My favorite show is coming on TV tonight, and Mom's cooking hamburgers. You know how I like her hamburgers. I can see if she can cook some for you. Can you come over here tonight?" asked Helen.

"No, I can't tonight. My mother wants to spend some time with me tonight. You know, quality-time stuff."

They both laughed because at times, quality time with their mothers was *bo*-ring. Once, Dee had spent some time with her mother, who tried to teach her how to knit. Dee tried to learn, but she didn't have the patience to sit still and work with those metal sticks. *I'd rather be playing football with Lance and Robert.*

Dee was athletic. She loved to play and watch sports. Her favorite was baseball; she could through a fast fastball. Her mother had played softball in school and liked to jog. Dee felt she'd gotten her love of sports from her mother though her mother had once told her that her father had played basketball in college.

Dee's mother told her quite a bit about her father, who was a kind and smart man. Dee couldn't understand why her father wasn't with them. Her mother always had a hard time explaining that and would change the subject; she'd say that was grown-up business. Her mother never said anything against her father. She always told her that her father loved her and that he always sent them money. Her mother also told her she sent him pictures of her.

"Where's he now?" she asked her mother.

"Spain," she answered. "You know he's in the air force. He's a pilot who flies jets. Someday, he'll come back to the States, and he said when he does, he'll come and visit you."

That was all her mother would say about her father. They never called or emailed each other. Dee didn't understand what was going on. She has a picture of him, a handsome man. I guess that it is grown-up business. *Maybe someday I'll see him, but my mother doesn't seem worried about it, so I won't worry about it either.*

Dee told Helen she would see her at the community center the next day.

"I'll come by your house, and we can ride down there together," said Helen.

"Okay, see you in the morning then," said Dee.

Helen hung up and went downstairs to the family room. She had a few minutes before dinner, so she turned on the TV and watched it until she heard her mother yell for her to come eat. The dinner table was all set; her mother was putting the finishing touches on the food. Her mother was a good cook and always insisted on eating fresh food. Her mother didn't eat out in restaurants much to Helen's dismay. Her mother didn't believe the food was of good quality; she would buy free-range meat because the animals weren't mistreated, and she thought the meat would be better because of that. She'd also buy organic fruit and vegetable at the co-op stores. "You are what you eat," she'd always say. "You eat quality food, you'll be a healthier person."

The hamburgers smelled delicious. Helen fetched ketchup and mustard and relish from the fridge. Her mother always made fresh french fries. It would be a great meal. And then, she'd curl up in her favorite quilt and watch TV. It was her turn to wash dishes that night, but she determined she'd get the dishes in the dishwasher as quickly as she could.

She sat down at the dinner table, and they said prayers. As her mother passed the hamburgers and buns, Helen asked, "Mom, can I leave early tomorrow to meet Dee so we can ride to the community center tomorrow?"

Her mother smiled. "Yes you can. I'm going to go to the co-op while you're at the community center, so make sure to take your house keys because I might not be home when you get back. And young lady, no company till I get home, understood?"

Helen nodded because she had a mouthful of food.

"You remember the last time you tried that, don't you?"

"Yes," Helen said. "I was on punishment for two weeks!" Helen thought about it and chuckled. "You have to admit, Mom. It was kind of funny, though.'"

Her mother giggled.

Helen remembered the day that Lance, Robert, and Dee had come over to her house to play. Even though Helen wasn't supposed to have company because her mother was working an hour late, she'd allowed her friends to come over. They'd raided the refrigerator and had made a mess making ham sandwiches, and they'd indulged in the chocolate chip cookies they'd found. Helen didn't know her mother had baked them for her coworkers.

They were in the middle of eating and watching TV when they had heard a car door close. "Everybody hide!" Helen yelled. Lance hid under the kitchen sink. Dee ran downstairs and hid in a pile of dirty clothes in the laundry room. Robert ran upstairs to hide underneath Helen's bed. All of them were holding their breaths when they heard the door open. Somehow, by the time Helen's mother reached the door, Helen had grabbed most of the mess and had hidden it under the kitchen sink, where Lance was hiding. Lance was covered with food, paper plates, and other garbage. He looked so funny with all that stuff on his head, but he was too scared to worry about that.

Helen ran to the family room and jumped on the sofa just as her mother entered the foyer. "Hello, Helen, where are you?"

"In the family room, Mom."

"You doing your homework?'"

"Yes I am." Helen was so scared that her mother would find her friends. Her mother put down her things and walked into the kitchen. Helen's heart was racing *Lance, please be very quiet.* Her mother went into the kitchen. Helen ran up to the bedroom and opened the window. "Robert?" she hissed.

"Underneath the bed," he whispered.

"Go out the window. There's a big tree branch out there. Go sit on it until I come and get you!" she whispered.

Robert got out from underneath the bed and looked out the window. "You must be crazy if you think I'm going to get into that tree!" He ran back and hid under the bed.

Helen sat on her bed. *I'm in big trouble!*

Meanwhile, Dee, in the basement, was wishing she had picked a warmer spot to hide. *My mother's going to call me soon, and if I'm not home, I'm in big trouble. I have to get out of here!*

Lance was trying his best not to sneeze. Helen's mother was in the kitchen humming. He was turning red from trying to hold his breath. He was just about to sneeze when Helen came into the kitchen. Her mother said, "I need to use the bathroom. I'll be right back." Helen leaned against the counter right when Lance let out a loud sneeze.

"Bless you," her mother said while in the bathroom.

Lance exited the kitchen cabinet wiping his nose. Helen let out a big laugh at the sight of Lance with all the garbage on him, but he was frowning. "Here, let me help you clean up" she whispered. "Then leave!"

Lance left out the backdoor. Helen quietly closed it so her mother wouldn't hear it. She hustled upstairs and told Robert to leave via the front door. Robert tiptoed out the bedroom, down the stairs, and out the door. Helen thought, *Two gone, one to go.* Just when Helen was going to go downstairs, her mother came out of the bathroom. "Helen, did I hear the front door open?" she asked.

"I was checking the mail for you."

"Did we get any today?"

"No we didn't." But Helen hadn't checked the mail at all. She was getting worried. Her mother headed downstairs to the basement. Helen tried to think of a way to stop her. "Mom! My head hurts bad!"

Her mother came up the stairs. At the same time, the phone rang. "You sit here while I answer that," her mother said.

Helen heard her mother pick up the phone. It was Dee's mother! She heard her mother say, "No, Dee isn't here. I haven't seen her today. Hold on a minute. Helen, have you seen Dee this afternoon?"

"Not since school."

"Didn't you two walk together from school today?"

"No. I had to talk to a teacher about a special homework assignment, and I was a little late, so I walked home by myself."

Helen was hoping that was a good enough explanation. She heard her mother repeat the answer she'd given and hang up. *Whew! Close one.*

Her mother yelled downstairs, "Helen, I'll look for some pain killer for your headache. I'll be down in a minute."

Helen ran to the basement. "Your mother is looking for you! Get out of here now!"

Dee whispered, "If I get into trouble because of this, I'm telling everything!"

Helen and Dee tiptoed up the stairs. They'd almost made it up the stairs to the backdoor when Helen's mother came into the kitchen. She put her hand on her hip. "What's going on here? Sit, young ladies. Dee, I'm going to call your mother, and we're going to get to the bottom of this!"

"I shouldn't have listened to you!" Dee hissed. "I'm in big trouble now. My mother will probably not let me go to the community center because of this, and you aren't going if I can't go!"

Helen knew Dee was right. They were in big trouble. Helen had lied to her mother.

Dee's mother arrived in five minutes, not looking happy. "Both of you are on punishment!" said Dee's mother. "We've already discussed it with each other."

Dee spilled out the whole story. The mothers were trying their best not to laugh. But when Dee said they had eaten all the cookies, Helen's mother wasn't pleased. When Helen found out they had been meant for her coworkers, she knew she was in even more trouble.

"Well young lady, you're going to help me bake another batch of cookies, and you're grounded!" Helen started to cry. It was a Friday. She wouldn't be able to go to the community center. What a fool she'd been for breaking the house rules.

Dee began to cry because she knew she was grounded too.

Helen's mother called Lance's and Robert's parents. It wouldn't be a fun week for any of them. "See what happens when you all don't respect our rules?" Helen's mother asked. "Go to your room, young lady. We still have to discuss the fact that you lied to me."

Helen, head bowed, left the kitchen as Dee and her mother were leaving. It was a bad day for all of them.

Lance's mother just shook her head when she saw his garbage-stained shirt. "Go upstairs, young man. Clean yourself up. I'm going to let your father handle this!"

Oh no! I'm grounded for sure!

Robert's father had answered the phone before Robert had made it home. "Thanks for calling me," he said to Helen's mother. "He hasn't gotten home yet. I'll be waiting."

When Robert got home, his father asked him why he was late from school.

"I had to do some extra homework, so I stayed at school to work in the library," Robert said.

Robert's dad face turned into an ugly frown. Robert knew his father knew that he was lying. "Let me explain, Dad—"

"No need to, Robert. I already know. I just got off the phone with Helen's mother. How did you think you were going to get away with lying to my face?"

Robert knew he'd be doing extra chores and it would be a no-go for going to the community center and riding his scooter.

"Hand over your iPod!"

"Dad, not the iPod!" Robert cried out, but he knew his father meant it. He went to get it. *I'm not talking to Helen for the rest of my life!*

"Go to your room right now. I'll deal with you later!"

Helen and her mother laughed as she remembered that situation. Helen's mother said, "I really hope that you learned your lesson!"

Helen said, "I'll always follow your rules, Momma. I know that was wrong, but you must admit it was funny!"

They laughed at the memory.

Dee was at home, bored. She wished she could spend the night with Helen. She went to her bedroom and sat in the bay window bench. The fall leaves were colorful. She watched the trees sway back and forth. Her mother was downstairs cooking. She always cooked from box dinners—sometimes good but other times icky. Dee wished her mother cooked like Helen's mother did. To Dee's surprise, her mother was making homemade pizza. She really liked her mother's pizza.

Her mother had rented some movies for them to see together. Sometimes, she would rent movies that were boring, but that night, she'd actually gotten some good ones.

"Come eat!"

Dee ran downstairs because she was hungry. While eating, Dee asked her mother if she could have some money for fuel for her scooter. "Dee, I'm broke until payday. I just went grocery shopping and paid some bills. Do you think your coach at the community center can help you out? I can pay him next Friday."

"Mom, we never have any money! Why is that?"

"You know everyone can't be rich, but we do have each other. I want more money too, but I'm doing the best I can. Your grandmother will send you some money next month, and I want you to spend it wisely."

"Hey! How much?"

"She said around a hundred dollars. I want you to put most of it into your savings account."

Dee hung her head. *She always wants me to put money in my savings account. I know we're supposed to save, but sometimes, I wish she'd let me buy what I wanted to buy!* "Can I spend some on fuel? We're practicing for the competition."

Her mother nodded. "You really like riding that scooter, don't you?"

"Yes I do, and I'm good at it."

"How long before the competition?"

Dee looked at the calendar. "Two weeks from this Saturday. I'm really excited, and our teams do some really good tricks. You're going to be surprised. Did you make sure you can get off that date?"

"Yes, I have that date off unless there are too many emergencies. Don't worry. I'll be there. I wouldn't miss this for the world!"

Dee smiled and hugged her mother. She helped her mother clean the kitchen, and then they watched the movies. It was a good evening after all.

Chapter 5

It was nine o'clock Saturday morning. Lance had showered and was putting on his favorite track outfit. It was comfortable, and he could ride the scooter with ease. He put on his old gym shoes because riding the scooter made his shoes dirty; he liked to keep his newer shoes for wearing to school.

"Breakfast is ready!" called out his mother.

"Coming down!"

His mother had made scrambled eggs, bacon, and toast. He was hungry. By the time he got there, his mother was pouring orange juice for him. His dad was still sleeping. He had worked long hours the day before and loved sleeping in on Saturdays.

"Is you scooter all ready for practice?" his mother asked.

"Yes. I worked on it a little yesterday. I put some detail tape on it, and it looks real cool, Mom."

Lance had put blue detailing tape on his silver scooter; he thought looks were as important in competition as the tricks they would perform. He was excited about the competition; he had worked hard on it. He wondered if he'd be able to do all the tricks without falling off. He had a trick no one had seen that he'd worked on after school and was excited about. "Mom, you and Dad will be there, right?"

"Why of course we'll be there. You've been working real hard on this. We wouldn't miss this for the world!"

Lance smiled. He looked at his watch. "I'm going in five minutes, Mom. I'll be back in about three hours."

"Okay. You be good, and be very careful. I know it's only two blocks away, but watch for traffic, and don't forget what the coach said. Ride on the side of the streets, and watch out for parked cars."

"I'll be careful, Mom. I don't want anything to happen to my scooter. You know the winner gets two hundred dollars, and I want that real bad!"

He wrapped the rest of his eggs and bacon in a piece of toast. He quickly swallowed his orange juice and kissed his mother good-bye. He ran out the kitchen door and into the garage for his scooter, which he pushed to the driveway. He finished his sandwich, started his scooter, and rode to Robert's house.

Robert was finishing up his cold cereal. Everybody else was still asleep. He'd set his alarm and gotten himself up. The house was quiet except for his brother's snoring. He had already showered and dressed. He liked getting himself ready; he felt he was old enough to do so, and it made him feel responsible. But his mother wouldn't let him cook by himself. She once said, "Child, you'd burn the house down and the food with it!"

Robert knew he couldn't cook very well, but he'd been watching his mother and felt he could do it. She hadn't taught him to cook though he'd repeatedly asked her. "When you turn thirteen, I'll teach you," she'd said.

"That's two years from now!"

"Yes, you're right. That's how old I was when I learned to cook."

Robert heard the doorbell. He ran to the front door and saw Lance. He told him he'd be out in a minute. He gobbled his cereal and grabbed his helmet. He ran to the side door that led to the garage and pressed the button to open the garage door. He started his red-and-silver scooter and rode out. He stopped the engine, laid the scooter down, and pushed the button to let the garage door down. He made sure the front door was locked and started his scooter again. They rode to Helen's house.

Helen was sitting on the front steps, her scooter right next to her. She saw the two boys coming and hopped on her scooter. She yelled to her mother that she was going and rode to the street, helmet on. Helen had drunk a yogurt smoothie for breakfast; she was watching her weight. She still wasn't as used to the scooter as she wanted to be, but she loved to ride it. She had signed up to be in the competition but knew she wouldn't win. She could do some tricks but needed to work on the harder ones.

The three rode to Dee's. She was sitting outside crying. They rode into her driveway and saw her scooter in the garage. "What's wrong with the scooter, Dee?" asked Helen.

Dee could hardly talk. "It won't start. It's not doing anything!"

Robert said, "Let me look at it." He tried to start it. Nothing. Not a sound. He worked with the wires, loosening one and tightening another. He tried to start the engine. It sputtered.

Dee stopped crying. She watched Robert work on the engine. He liked working with his hands, and he had watched his father work on his scooter. He figured even though it was low on fuel, it should get her there. Robert tried it again. The scooter started, and everyone yelled, "Yes!"

Dee's mother came out and saw that Robert had fixed the engine. "Thank you so much, Robert. You're quite a young man!"

Dee kissed Robert on his cheek; he grinned from ear to ear. They all waved good-bye to Dee's mother.

"Be careful and remember the rules of safety!" she yelled above the loud engines.

They headed down the street. They were happy and smiling, especially Dee. She wanted to be in the competition real bad. She'd ask the coach to look at her scooter when she got to the community center; he would make sure it was safe. She had on kneepads as well as her helmet. She had a special trick to practice for the competition. She wasn't scared to do difficult stunts on her scooter. Her coach was always telling her to be careful. He'd said some tricks were too dangerous for her to do, but she wasn't scared at all.

Old Man Davis was working in his garden. The sounds of the little engines broke the morning's silence. *Those kids again. Why do they have to be so loud? But they're good kids, and I guess the noise will be gone soon.*

"Good morning Mr. Davis!" yelled Robert as he passed.

He looked up, waved, and turned back to his gardening. *It'll soon turn cold, and I'll have to stop working in this garden.*

But for now, it's still warm, and the flowers are still blooming. If the wife were still here, she'd be working with me.

He was lonely; he had lost his wife just a year ago. He liked having the children around, especially Robert. He thought there was something special about that child. He thought he was very well mannered and nice. Robert didn't know it, but Old Man Davis had put a little money aside for his education. He thought Robert did such a good job when he raked his lawn. He didn't have any children. *Why not give a little money for Robert's college education?* He wouldn't tell him about it for a year. *This neighborhood has always helped each other, and Robert is a good soul. Besides, his mother cooks a mean sweet potato pie.*

About thirty students were in the citywide competition. Lance and Robert had tried for the first time last year but hadn't won. Helen had just gotten her scooter and would compete this year. Dee had won third place last year and was shooting for first place this year. They lived for the competition.

As they rode to the community center, Robert decided it was time for some music, so he put his iPod on his belt and placed the earphones on his head.

"Oh oh, Robert has the earphones on!" Dee hollered.

"Yeah, he's getting ready to seriously ride!" said Lance.

"I worry he won't hear the traffic," said Helen.

"I can hear you. Don't worry about me!" Robert said.

It was clear but chilly. Lance wished he'd worn his heavier jacket. Helen had a scarf and gloves because she'd watched the weather the night before—cold in the morning but around sixty the rest of the day.

Dee wore her heavier jacket because her mother had insisted. "You know how you are. One sneeze and you're sick for a week or two, so cover up, young lady."

They all noticed how quiet it was. On school day mornings, the streets were busy with cars, trucks, and buses. Birds were chirping. Dee thought, *This is a great morning to ride our scooters. It's just us on the road.* The others must have been thinking the same thing because no one was speaking, just riding.

"Helen, have you been practicing your tricks?" Lance asked.

Helen looked back at Lance. "Real hard, but I'm scared of trying the loop to loop. It frightens me!"

"Why didn't you ask me to help you out?"

"Because I need to learn it by myself. What can you do to help me with that?"

"We have a trampoline. If you can do a flip on it, you wouldn't be scared."

"I didn't think about that!"

"How about coming over tomorrow?" Lance asked. "I'll have my dad spot for us. I'll teach you how to flip forward and back. You'll be an ace at it, and then you won't be scared to do the loop to loop on your scooter."

Helen was excited about that. "You'd do that for me?"

Lance had had a secret crush on her since he was six, but he'd always been too shy to tell her. He was afraid she wouldn't talk to him if she knew. He was hoping she would date him when they got older. But for the time being, he just liked being near her and being her friend.

Helen had never given it much thought too much. She remembered he'd been a funny-looking kid with braces, but since the braces had come off, she realized he was a good-looking boy. Helen liked him, but just as a friend. He was always there to tell her things would be all right. He was like a big brother to her.

When Helen father's left almost a year earlier, she'd had horrible feelings. She missed her father so much but couldn't tell anyone how she felt. One day, she was sitting on her porch crying her eyes out. Her mother was napping, so she didn't want to wake her up. She thought she was a big crybaby. Her hands were covering her eyes; she had her dad's picture he had given her lying next to her. She was remembering all the things they used to do together—trips out of town, going for ice cream cones, and talking. Life was really good when her dad was around. She was scared he'd get hurt. Her feelings were so mixed up; she didn't know how to fix them.

She felt something very soft on her arm. She looked up slowly because it kind of scared her. Someone was pushing a pink stuffed bunny at her arm. It was Lance.

"I'm sorry your father's in Iraq," he said. "I hope this bunny will help you sleep better."

"Oh, Lance! You're my best friend!" She hugged him. "Thank you so much! You knew I was sad!"

Lance had saved money for something else, but when he heard Helen's father had gone to war, he wanted to get her something.

I'll never forget what Lance did for me. He's so kind. And I thought her was a nerd! She chuckled.

They were almost at the community center. They saw about twelve kids on scooters heading that way too. Robert picked up speed when he saw a friend he hadn't seen in a while. *Whoa! He was sick a while ago, but look at him now!* "Hey man, where've you been?" The two of them met at the obstacle course and began to talk.

Dee caught up with Helen. "Helen, can I spend the night with you tonight?"

"Is your mother working late again? She didn't call my mother."

"I'm not sure if she's working late or not. I just wanted to sleep over again. I had fun, and that bed was so nice," Dee said with a big smile. "We can ask her when we get home. Maybe we can have a slumber party, just you and me." Dee smiled. She liked Helen, and she always liked the treats her mother would buy for sleepovers. "If she says yes, I'll ask my mother to buy us some treats too." Dee loved to eat. Cheeseburgers and french fries, she couldn't get enough. She thought that if she owned a burger joint, she'd probably go out of business because she'd eat all the burgers herself. She also liked cake, lots of it. When her birthday came, her mother would buy those bakery cakes. White cake was her favorite; she'd eat that like it was going out of style. Then she'd always ask her mom, "Why did you let me eat all the cake?"

"Because it's your birthday! I let you do what you want."

"Dee, stop daydreaming or you'll crash!" Helen said.

Dee woke up from her daydream just in time to steer her scooter away from the curb. "Thanks, Helen."

The coach watched the children ride up. He had coached the scooter competition for years. He loved to watch the children develop their personal tricks, but he was also responsible for their safety while they were there. He had strict rules the children had to abide by or they wouldn't be allowed to ride the obstacle course. He'd always say, "If you don't follow my rules, go home!" No one played with the coach. He'd raised two sons and two daughters, all going to college then. They were smart. He always told the children that education was the only way to make it in this world, and he always pushed everyone to do their best.

He used to play baseball and had almost made it to the majors before an injury stopped him. He said he was heartbroken. He went to college and majored in sports. He taught school and coached baseball; his team did pretty well. He still taught, but part-time. He wanted to help the neighborhood kids, so he volunteered at the community center. He said volunteering to teach others was more rewarding than getting paid for it, and he wanted the kids to consider the community center to be their safe place.

His wife had passed away a few years earlier, so he had time on his hands. He wanted to prepare all the youth for the competition; he had to make sure that they knew all the safety rules, that they had all their equipment on, and that their jumps weren't too difficult for them. He'd told them, "You can be as creative as you want, but you must be able to do the main jumps as perfectly as you can because that's what the judges are looking for. Most of you can do some very good jumps, but I'm concerned for your safety, so if any of the fancy stuff looks too hazardous, I'll tell you not to do them."

He was concerned about Dee, who had no fear. She'd been upset the previous year when she got third place. He worried about some other too he thought didn't recognize their limits.

"Okay, secure your scooters and come inside for orientation to this year's competition. After you hear what we have to say, you can practice for three hours tops. Then you all go home or lock up your scooters if you're going stay around for other activities. That clear?"

"Yes," everyone but Robert said. He was still on his iPod.

The coach made him turn it off. "I need for you to be alert and hear the orientation information, young man."

Robert frowned but understood and turned off the music. He knew he had a good chance of placing in the top four and didn't want the coach upset with him.

Dee and Helen sat together. Dee saw that Helen was nervous. "Why are you so worried? It's going to be okay. You have all your safety equipment, so you won't hurt yourself, right?"

"I'm not worried about hurting myself. I'm worried about the loop to loop."

"We'll practice it today. Have you ever done it before?"

Helen shook her head. "Lance said he was going to teach me to flip on the trampoline, and that should help."

"Good idea. I'll come over too. We can both help you. Who's going to spot for us?"

"Lance said he'd ask his father. I'll ask my mother if she can help spot too."

After the orientation, the children filed out of the gym. Dee told Helen, "I thought I was going to sleep in there! I'm sure glad that's over."

Helen looked at the obstacle course and wished her father were there to coach her and tell her everything would work out just fine. She was always a little braver when he did that. She rolled her scooter to the line. Eleven other children were competing. Some were so good that Helen knew she would never place, but some were average, as she was. She had just started the previous summer and hadn't had the opportunity to practice like the rest of the kids. *Maybe I can place if I work extra hard.*

"You ready to do this?" Lance asked her.

Helen smiled. "You better teach me how to do the loop to loop."

"I've already asked my father about spotting, and he said it will have to be tomorrow afternoon when we get back from church."

"Okay. I'll ask my mother to help spot too. Dee wants to come over. That okay?"

"Sure. Why not? She can help show you. She's not scared of anything!"

"Thanks, Lance. You're a good friend."

It was Dee's turn to practice. She was excellent on the obstacle course. She had her own tricks she added to the program. She glided through the orange cones with such ease. She also liked to put her feet up in the air and let the scooter take her away. Her personal trick was standing on the seat and letting go of the handlebars for a few seconds. No one else could do that, and the coach told the others that Dee was the only one who should.

The other children had their turns and did pretty well. One kid fell down after doing a loop to loop. Helen shuddered at the thought of that happening to her. The coach ran over to see if he was all right. He was. Thank goodness he'd had his helmet on.

No one had received bad injuries while doing the obstacle course. The coach stated it was because they were wearing the proper padding and helmets. He wouldn't let anyone on the course unless they had the proper equipment.

Robert's turn came up. He had his own tricks too, and he was really good. He went through the course with no problem. He did a perfect loop to loop that was sweet to watch. Helen applauded him. *Dee, Lance, and Robert are so good at it*, she thought. She wondered if she should even be in the competition, but in her heart, she wanted to try.

That was it. She was up next. She took a deep breath and got on her scooter. She handled it well; she went through most of the obstacle course with no problems. She was a little slower than the others, but she did each move perfectly. The coach didn't want them to rush particularly if they were nervous.

The loop to loop was the last stunt before riding out on a straight course. Helen saw it coming. She looked at it and couldn't bring herself to do it. She swerved around the loop to loop and went on the straight course. Some of the other children chuckled, but the coach told her, "Don't worry, Helen. I'm proud that you did most of the course, and it was perfect. When you gain your confidence, you'll master the loop to loop." He patted her on the back and motioned for another student to come up.

Lance was up last, and his routine was perfect. He had his own tricks and did everything so well. He had a trick where he'd get off the scooter, run alongside it for a few seconds, and jump back on—a trick no one else could do. Everyone applauded when he was finished. He bowed. "Thank you, Thank you!"

Everyone laughed, including the coach. "Okay, superstar, you know you're good, don't you?" He laughed and walked away.

One girl, from Somali, was real nice. Her parents wouldn't allow her to take off her head covering, and they didn't want her to do the tricks either, but she had begged her parents to let her try. They finally gave in. She found a way to don her helmet and pads. She could wear jeans; she just couldn't let her hair show. She was very good. She wasn't afraid, and she did all the tricks. Her family was watching and was very surprised when she completed the obstacle course. They jumped up and down yelling her name. Everyone knew she had done something very special. All in all, it was a very good practice.

When it was over, Lance, Robert, Dee, and Helen rode home. They didn't want to stay for the other activities; they were still worked up about the competition, and they were very tired. On the way home, they made a pit stop at a coffee shop for custard ice cream cones. The shop owner saw them coming. "Here come the kids," she said to the other workers. "Let's get the cones ready."

The four would sit on their scooters as they ate the cold custard. "This has to be the best ice cream in town!" said Lance. The others nodded, too busy eating to talk.

It was a nice coffee shop. Adults would stop by and read books or newspapers. It looked like a living room inside with coaches, tables, and chairs. The children didn't go inside because they didn't want their scooters stolen. Lance remembered one time that his father had gone there for coffee. His mother had gotten upset with his father, and this was where his father hung out to "get some peace of mind," he'd say.

After they finished, they rode home. It had been a busy morning. When Lance got home, he asked his mother if he could take a nap before his chores. She told him that was okay. Lance ran upstairs, took a shower, and snuggled under his covers. He was asleep in minutes.

When Helen got home, her mother was getting ready to shop for groceries. "Is it all right if I nap while you shop?"

Her mother saw she was tired. "Okay, but don't let anyone in, and only answer the cell phone. I'll put it on your nightstand."

"Okay, Momma, I promise."

Her mother left, and Helen went straight to bed. *I'll take a bath when I get up.* She fell asleep in minutes.

Robert wasn't tired at all. He considered it a workday. He planned to see if anyone needed anything done. He'd always get a newspaper for one older woman down the street; she'd always give him two dollars. And he planned to see if the woman with three kids needed anything from the store. Sometimes, she'd give him five dollars to get some baby formula. And of course his best customer was Old Man Davis, who always had something for him to do. He liked that old man even though at times he seemed a little mean. Robert thought it was because his legs ached all the time from working so much in his garden.

Robert put his earphones on and cranked up the music as he walked down the street looking for work; he was always thinking about making money. Old Man Davis had told him, "Someday, you're going to be very successful!" Robert sure hoped he was right.

Dee had some chores, including cleaning her room, a big mess too. She wished she had kept it clean. Her mother told her that if she picked up a little bit every day, she wouldn't have to worry about picking up on the weekends. She wondered why she never listened to her mother's advice. Her mother had told her, "I'm not going to pick up your room for you anymore. You're a big girl now. It's your responsibility to keep your room clean." *What a mess!* she thought as she looked over her room. *But I'm so tired!*

She began putting her dirty clothes in a pile. Pretty soon, she was lying on top of the pile snoring away.

Chapter 6

I t was Saturday evening, and it was quiet in the neighborhood. The day had been warm and sunny. Most of the neighbors were on their porches talking to each other and admiring each other's lawns and gardens. Lance was lying in his yard looking up and watching squirrels jump from tree to tree. He felt so lazy and hungry. His dad was grilling steaks outside, and they smelled great. He liked his neighborhood. Nothing bad ever happened there. It was a safe place. All the neighbors knew each other and helped each other with everything. All the kids knew each other also. Some of his former babysitters were in college. *Boy, did they grow up fast!* he thought.

Dee and her mother were eating dinner. Dee had prepared the salad. This was after her mother had found Dee snoring away on her pile of dirty clothes. "Dee! Wake up! Clean that room right now!" her mother had told her.

Dee remembered how she had jumped up from a very relaxing sleep. "Sorry, Momma. I fell asleep. I'll get it cleaned. Don't worry!" Dee had immediately begun to clean her room, and her mother had given her a smile and went downstairs to put up the groceries.

That girl! But she's a good girl, and I love her so, her mother had thought.

During dinner, she asked her mother if she'd like to go shopping the next day.

"You know I'm a little short of money, young lady."

"I have twenty dollars saved up," Dee said. "I want to get a T-shirt for the competition. Can you take me to a discount store?"

Her mother looked at Dee lovingly. "Yes, we can go tomorrow."

"Can we go early? Oh, yeah, I need to ask you something else. Helen needs to learn how to back and forward flip on the trampoline. Lance's father is going to be one spotter. Can you be the other?"

"Why does she need to learn that?"

"Lance thinks if she's not afraid to do the back and forward flips, she'll be able to do the loop to loop on the obstacle course. She's scared to do it right now."

"Makes sense. We better go to the store early so we can get back to help her out."

Dee hugged her mother. Sometimes, they'd get mad at each other. Mainly, it was Dee getting mad at her mother, but she knew that she had a good mother who worked hard at the hospital to give her a good home. She thought her mother was a strong person, but she wished her mother had a boyfriend because she thought her mother was lonely. Her mother had told her, "If I'm meant to have a boyfriend, one will come. I'm not looking right now. I'm happy." Sometimes, though, her mother looked sad when she saw couples holding hands. She sometimes wished her father would show up and take care of them, but she knew better. A new man in her mother's life would be good as long as he treated her well.

They continued to eat and talk until it got dark. Then they did their usual—watched a movies and had popcorn and sodas.

Helen had woken up and had taken a shower. Her mother had also gone grocery shopping, so she helped her put the groceries up. She started to flip water from her still-wet hair on her mother. "Hey now! Stop that, young lady!" Her mother scooped some water from the faucet and threw it at Helen, who yelped and ran to the living room. Her mother laughed. *I really needed a laugh!* She chased Helen and gave her a big hug.

"Guess what? I heard from your father today. He told me he might come home sooner than expected!"

"Really, Momma? That's wonderful! Did he say when?"

"No, he just said it could be soon. Wouldn't that be something?"

Her mother was so happy. Helen hoped it would be soon. They had tried to keep up the house, but there were some things a man needed to do. Helen remembered when her mother had tried to clean the gutters but finally hired someone to do that, something her father used to do all the time.

Helen would be so glad to see her father. She hoped he'd let them know when he was coming so they could get the house decorated and have friends over. *I could bake a cake and help Momma make his favorite foods.*

"How was the obstacle course today?" her mother asked.

"I had a hard time again. I did everything right except that old loop to loop!"

"I'm confident that someday you'll do it. For now, just be happy you did the rest correctly."

"Lance and Dee are going to show me how to do a back and forward flip on the trampoline tomorrow. Lance says I'll get used to flying in the air and then I won't be scared to do it."

Her mother frowned. "You sure you want to learn that?"

"Yes I am, Momma. Lance's father will spot for us, and I think Dee's mother is going to also."

"I want to be there to catch you in case you flip too far out!"

They laughed and hugged.

"Help me with the dishes," her mother said.

They cleaned up the kitchen and got on the Internet to email her father. Helen liked to keep him updated on what she was doing. He was her best friend next to her mother and Lance. She liked to hear what he was doing in Iraq. She was sure he didn't tell her too much about the bad stuff, though he had told her he'd been scared a couple of times. She always prayed he wouldn't get hurt. She felt her prayers were being answered because so far, he was okay.

After they got off the Internet, her mother knitted as Helen watched TV. Her mother always had to approve what she was watching. Sometimes, Helen would get frustrated because she wanted to see music videos but her mother would tell her no. There was no changing her mother's mind about it, so she'd pick what she wanted to see and get her mom's okay.

Robert had gotten home right before dusk. His little sister was in the bathroom. "Hey! When you coming out?"

"Go use the other one! I'm going to be here for a while"

Oh boy. I know what that means. He ran downstairs to use the bathroom by the kitchen. His mother was preparing dinner as his father was reading the newspaper as usual. *I wish he'd get his nose out of that paper and talk to me sometimes!*

Just as he was thinking that, a surprising thing happened. "Hey, son. I talked to the coach at the community center today, and he said you're very good on the obstacle course. Well done!"

Robert was so surprised he couldn't say anything. His father had actually taken time out to say something good to him. He and his mother were shocked.

"I'm proud of you, son. Just wanted to let you know. Sometimes, I don't say it as much as I should. I love my entire family," his father said.

Is my father okay?

His mother had had the same thought and asked her husband if he was okay.

"Sure I'm okay! Can't a father compliment his son?"

His mother smiled and hugged her husband.

"Where's our daughter?" he asked.

"In the bathroom," Robert said.

"That child can stay in there forever," Robert's mother said with a laugh. "She just got a new magazine, and it'll be a long time!"

Father and son laughed as well.

Robert told his father about his day after the practice at the center and that he had made twenty dollars. He had shopped for the woman with three children, took out the garbage for an elderly neighbor, and swept Old Man Davis's driveway.

His father was always surprised at how much money Robert earned doing chores. "You remind me of your grandfather. He'd do odd jobs and make a lot of money. Keep up the good work, son."

Robert's older came home from football practice. He looked tired. "Hey, bro!" Robert yelled.

"Hey bro to you too!" he said on his way to the shower.

He beat me to the shower again! Now both bathrooms are being used! Robert thought as he headed to his room to change. But he liked his family; he considered them cool. He lay on his bed and waited for dinner. He dozed off.

About a half hour later, Robert's mother called out, "Robert! Come down and eat your dinner before it gets cold! Everyone's already eaten!"

Robert stretched. "Down in a minute, Mom!" *I didn't know I was that tired.* He got downstairs in a couple of minutes. He was hungry for the fried chicken and mashed potatoes and gravy he knew his mom had made. His favorites. He wasn't that crazy about the tossed salad, but he ate until he couldn't eat any longer. He barely had room for the strawberry shortcake with whipped cream, but he managed that.

His mother told him he'd better enjoy the strawberries because winter was coming and they wouldn't have them again till summer. His mother was known throughout the neighborhood for her desserts. She'd always cook for neighbors who were sick or who had suffered some kind of loss; she was kindhearted like that. She once said, "Good things will come to you if you do good deeds."

After dinner, he went to the family room, where everyone was lying around looking full. It was a funny sight to Robert. "Hey, what movies are we looking at tonight?" he asked. "How about some sci-fi?"

His sister frowned. "I want something funny!"

Robert's father let out a big yawn. "I'm going to take a hot bath and go to bed. I had a long week."

"I think I'll join you," his wife said.

Robert's older brother smiled. "Are you going to have some quality time?"

They rolled their eyes and headed to their room. "You children behave," she said. "We can hear what's going on. No fighting over the movies or I'll turn the TV off!"

After they left, the children started wrestling for the remote. "Let me have it!" yelled Robert's little sister, but he had a good grasp on it and just played with his sister. She was getting mad, but he liked to tease her. He enjoyed it when her eyes got big and she put her hands on her hips. She wasn't afraid of him. She was strong; she had to be to tussle with her brothers. No one else could tease her. They were always protective of her and wouldn't let bullies at school bother her. Sometimes, they would walk her to school and home, Robert and his brother taking turns at that. Robert considered himself her guardian; he wasn't about to let her get jumped on by anyone.

He finally let go of the remote control as he was laughing. He was holding his stomach because he was so full. His older brother was laughing too. His sister was breathing hard because she'd used so much energy to wrestle with her brother. "You just wait until I'm as big as you!" she said. "I'll show you!"

"Yeah, right," said Robert. "I'll be waiting."

Chapter 7

The next day, which was Sunday, most of the families went to church, but Robert fought going. The pastor was so boring that even Robert's father would fall asleep and snore in church. It was the funniest thing. His head would get to bobbing, and his mouth would open, and just when the pastor was getting ready to say a prayer, Robert's father would let out a loud snore. His mother would pinch his leg, and he'd wake up suddenly and shout, "Amen!" which made the whole church laugh.

Robert's mother would be so embarrassed, Robert would sink into his seat, and the pastor would frown at the idea anyone would fall asleep during his good sermon. He'd go every Sunday and would fall asleep every time, but he wasn't the only husband who snoozed off, much to their wives' dismay.

But Robert, his sister, and his brother would crack up every time. Their mother would give them stern looks, but they couldn't help themselves. The ride home would be quiet; no one was talking because their father had made their mother mad. *Church is funny*, Robert thought. *It's worth getting up and going just to see my father snore and embarrass himself!*

Dee also went to church with her mother, and if her mother had to work, her mom's best friend would take her. Dee liked going with the best friend because she'd always take her for ice cream later. She was just like an aunt to Dee; she didn't have any children, so she'd spoil Dee. "You mustn't buy so much for Dee," her mother would tell her friend. "She's getting spoiled!"

And her friend would always say, "But you were spoiled by my mother when we were kids. I'm just doing what comes naturally!"

They'd both laugh. Her mother really didn't mind the kindness because she was raising a child alone; anything her friend gave her and Dee was greatly appreciated.

Dee always wondered why her mother's friend wasn't married. She once told Dee, "My knight in shining armor hasn't come yet!" Dee told her that someday she'd get married. "You'll certainly be in the wedding," the friend had told Dee. "I'm in no rush, though. I'm always happy to see you and your mother. You two are my best friends!"

Dee blushed. She really likes her mother's friend; they had gone to school together just as she and Helen were doing. She hoped their friendship would last as long as her mother's and her friend's had. And Dee liked getting all the gifts too.

Church was okay, but the reverend was so boring; Dee thought she'd go to sleep. She asked her mother's friend how she liked it. "It was okay, but I thought he was too dry today."

"So did I!" said Dee. "He always talks about sports. Basketball last Sunday and today football."

They laughed. Dee told her mother's friend that she had to get home by one because she was going to help Helen learn the backflip. Her mother's friend thought that was nice. "We better get going then," she said. "You don't want to be late."

They left for Dee's home. Dee thought her mother would be home by the time they got there. She had to work the morning shift at the hospital and had said she should be home by the time church let out.

Helen didn't go to church. Her mother had said she didn't have to go every Sunday. She guessed her mother didn't want to go to church because people would constantly ask her about her dad, which would sadden her mother. "You know, since your father is in Iraq, we don't need to go to church that much until he gets home."

Helen had said, "That's all right with me! I don't like getting up so early and dressing up to see a boring man preach."

"Now Helen, that's not what I meant. You can go with Dee sometime if you want."

"No, I'll just stay her with you."

Helen was glad because that meant she had more time to sleep; she didn't get up until ten. She felt she had the best mattress in town, and her pillows were made of foam that molded to her head and neck; she loved those pillows. And she had names for all the stuffed animals on her bed that she'd gather around her.

"Mom, just to remind you, I'm going to Lance's. He's going to teach me to backflip, remember?"

"Yes, I'd like to come with. Would you mind if I was a spotter? We can go out to eat afterward. I don't feel like cooking today."

Helen liked going out to eat with her mother; she immediately nodded to her mother's wanting to come and going out to dinner. "I think your being there will help me do this. I'm a little scared of going on the trampoline."

"I think you're a brave young lady for doing this. Just watch. It'll be fun, and you won't be scared this Saturday. I bet you'll do the loop to loop after today!"

She hugged her mother. "I love you, Mom. You know just what to say!"

Helen went to take her shower while her mother cleaned up the kitchen. Her mother was getting a little excited about the competition, but she knew her daughter was worried about it. She remembered when Helen asked her and her husband if she could get a scooter. She'd worried Helen might hurt herself. All three of them had gone to the coach, and he explained the program to them. Afterward, she felt a little better about allowing Helen to ride the scooter.

The police department, which considered a scooter a motor vehicle, approved of the program as long as adults handled the fuel and the children followed very strict riding rules. The community center developed the rules, which parents had to sign off on. The coach had to give the police a list of all children in the scooter program. The students received licenses for their scooters. They could ride them only to the community center or other places the coach approved of. If the kids broke the rules, their parents were obligated to take the scooters away and return the license to the coach.

Also, the children had to have a B or above average on their report cards, which they had to show the coach. "No exceptions!" he'd told them; he was very strict about grades, and the children knew that.

The children studied hard because the scooter practices were fun. At times, the coach would take them on field trips to other obstacle courses. The kids loved the program.

Helen's mother felt she'd made the right decision in letting Helen participate. She figured it kept her busy, and she was hanging out with friends who had grown up with her, which was nice. She finished the kitchen, picked up more in the house, took a shower, and got ready to spot for her daughter.

Lance did go to church. His family went every Sunday; they were very involved in the church. Lance was a junior usher and would pass the collection plate. But he also thought church was boring that day. He listened to the reverend talk about how money could help the needy, but he knew the congregation had bought him a new car. *Why was that? I mean, did he really need a new car? That reverend is supposed to work like the rest of us, but all he does is stand at the pulpit and blah, blah, blah.*

He didn't understand church, but his family loved the reverend. Lance liked to go on church field trips and to church picnics, but he didn't like sitting and having to listen to the reverend stuff. As he'd pass the collection plate, he'd notice people who looked like they were about to fall asleep, mostly children and men. Wives and mothers would pinch or nudge husbands and children, which made Lance chuckle though he tried to stifle it.

His mother whispered to his father, "Just look at your son laughing at those people!"

His father stifled a chuckle too. "I can't blame him. Just look at the some of the men whose heads are bobbing. It's funny. The reverend's sermon is really boring today."

Lance was almost done passing the collection plate. *I'll be glad when church is out.*

After the concluding sermon, the choir sang the usual closing hymn accompanied by the piano and marched out. The reverend said one more prayer, which was too long. *This is real torture!* Lance thought. People were wiggling in their seats as if in agreement.

When the reverend said, "Amen!" everyone seemed to get up at once and hustle to the doors. Men were loosening their ties, taking off their jackets, and scurrying to their cars, a funny sight to Lance. He himself ran to his father's SUV; he couldn't wait to get home and teach Helen how to backflip. *I'm going to make sure she can to the loop to loop. This'll be fun!*

He saw his father and mother talking to some other church members. *Don't they see I'm in a hurry?* He ran back and tugged on his father's jacket. "Dad, come on! We have to go. I told Helen to be there at one!"

"We're going, don't worry, son. We have plenty of time. I've already set up the trampoline, and the equipment is ready."

Lance calmed down a bit but was still anxious. Sometimes, he'd get all wound up for nothing. He just felt that things should always be on track and that they should get home.

Finally, his father and mother said good-bye to the people they were talking to and headed for the SUV. When they got home, Lance raced upstairs to get out of his church clothes and into his gym clothes. He hated dressing up, something he considered a real pain.

He was putting on his gym shoes when the phone rang. He heard his father say, "Yes, we're home. Lance said you'd be here at one."

Lance ran downstairs. "Was that Helen?"

"Yes. She'll be here in ten minutes. Let's check out the equipment."

Lance and his father went outside while his mother watched from the kitchen window. *They'll be thirsty and hungry after all the jumping around. I'll make some lemonade and get some cheese, crackers, and apples slices out.*

Lance's father used to be a gymnast and would practice flips on the trampoline; he was still good at it. Lance admired his father, but he'd been surprised when he said he would help Helen. Lance hadn't thought his father would make time for that, but right then he knew his father loved him.

Dee arrived at one with her mother's best friend. Lance's mother answered the door. "Come in! How are you two doing? Lance and his father are in the backyard checking on the equipment. You can go through the kitchen and to the backdoor."

"Is Helen here yet?" Dee asked.

"No, not yet," Lance's mother said.

They went to the backyard; Dee introduced her mother's friend to Lance's father. "My mother will be here soon," said Dee. "She wanted to help spot for Helen."

"The more the merrier!" Lance's father said. He was in good spirits.

Lance thought, *Maybe church is good for people. My dad's being real nice.*

Helen and her mother came into the backyard. They were impressed with the trampoline. Helen also looked at the large steel frame hanging over it. "What's that?"

"A training device," Lance said. "We'll put a belt on you that has a rope attached. In case you're about to fall off the trampoline, my dad can stop that and put you back on your feet!"

Helen looked at Lance. "You sure I'll be okay?"

Lance smiled. "You'll be just fine."

Robert showed up with his father. "We all came to spot for Helen!" Robert's father said.

"I really appreciate what you're doing for Helen," Helen's mother said.

Lance's father said, "You know you're a good neighbor. We always watch out for each other. Besides, I can teach her real quick."

Lance's father sat on the grass and motioned to Helen to do the same. He'd bought some training socks for her. "These are special socks. They have grips underneath that will help you not slip when you land on your feet. Lance, warm the trampoline," he yelled. "You'll need two spotters," he told Helen.

Dee's mother and her best friend volunteered to spot. Lance got on the trampoline, rolled away the safety bar, and began to jump up and down. Lance had mastered the trampoline; his father had trained him when he was little. His father thought he could also be a gymnast, especially on the trampoline. Lance was an excellent flipper. His father had taught him a routine.

Helen looked at Lance with amazement. *He's wonderful! Look how he can do those flips and he not scared!* She watched him do perfect triple flips. Everyone but the spotters applauded; they were concentrating on Lance, who would fly so high that it scared her.

Dee's mother and her friend had been cheerleaders and had also practiced on the trampoline. They knew the rules about spotting and were very serious about it; they had had to protect their friends while they were flipping. Helen was glad to see they were good spotters.

Lance came off the trampoline and went inside for some water; his routine was difficult, and he hadn't done it in a long time.

"You okay, Lance?" his mother asked.

"Yes, just tired after that workout. It's been a while!" He ran out to help Helen into her safety belt.

Helen was excited. She'd of course jumped on her bed, but this was way different. "Lance, you were real good! Do you think I could be that good?"

"Of course! You just need training. Today, you'll learn to flip backward and forward. That'll get you used to how it feels to do the loop to loop. It feels like a flip."

Lance's father said, "I'll make sure the belt is fastened properly. That's my job." He fastened the belt and made sure it was secure. "Too tight?" he asked. Helen told him it was okay. "Then let's get started, young lady. Up you go." Lance's father hoisted her up to the trampoline. "Okay, everyone around the trampoline to spot."

Everyone did. Helen was a little scared, but she was determined to learn. She wanted to do the loop to loop the next Saturday—now or never. She followed Lance's father's instructions. First, she just jumped up and down; he wanted her not to be scared about jumping. He told her to jump a little higher. Then he told her to act like she was going to jump off the trampoline; he wanted her to know he could stop her. She tried it a couple of times, and each time, Lance's father had her; she realized he wouldn't let her fall.

But her mother was a little scared. When she first tried it, she almost let out a scream. It was scary to watch, but she saw Helen was becoming comfortable with it. She remembered when she'd tried her first flip, when she was about five. It had been scary at first, but she became very good at it. She was glad her daughter was gaining confidence and learning something new. She wished her father were there to his brave daughter. She smiled at her daughter to give her encouragement.

Lance was proud of her as well. He thought she'd be crying and screaming, but Helen was doing pretty well and looked like she was enjoying herself. Lance's father told her he wanted her to jump a little higher, so she did, and she felt like a bird. She was jumping so high that she could see over some of the smaller trees in Lance's yard. *I thought I'd be scared, but I'm not!*

Lance's father told her how to properly stop a jump; she followed his instructions and did. "Rest for a minute. You'll practice jumping up and down while tucking your feet up. Tuck them as close to your body as you can. Do that about three times."

They waited until she was ready; she started jumping again. The tucks were easy for her. She was very flexible. *This is cool!*

Lance's father told her how to do a forward flip. "Do it exactly as I told you."

She followed his instructions. The first flip was scary. She went over toward the side, but Lance's father tugged on the rope and kept her from landing on the ground. Lance's father noticed Helen's mother's anxiety. "Don't worry," he said. "She'll be fine. Just let her do it a couple of times."

Helen tried it three times and finally completed a forward flip. Everyone yelled and clapped to congratulate her. *I did it!* It was the first time in her life that she'd tried something so adventurous. *What have I been afraid of?* "I want to try it again, please."

"You're the boss!" Lance's father said. Helen did it again and again.

"You feel comfortable now?" Lance's father asked, and Helen nodded. "Then we'll try a backflip." Helen was a little scared; she felt she'd not be able to see where her feet landed, but Lance's father gave her pointers on how to measure her landing. "Don't worry. I won't let you land on your head." He laughed.

Lance's father was an excellent teacher; he loved to teach tricks on the trampoline. He'd thought about teaching children a while ago but didn't do it because of his work.

Helen tried a backflip and almost landed on her head. Her mother was scared of this stunt; she remembered how scared she'd been when she was learning. But she looked at her daughter and gave her a smile to signal she was behind her and everything would be okay. "Try it again baby," she yelled. "You can do it."

Helen smiled and began jumping again. She followed the instructions Lance's father was yelling at her. His voice gave her confidence; she trusted what he was saying. She jumped higher. When Lance's father gave the word, she attempted a backflip and nailed it. Everyone was jumping. Helen's mother was holding her mouth with her hands and crying tears of joy for her brave daughter.

Lance's father yelled, "All right!" Dee was jumping up and down with her mother. Her mother's best friend was also proud of Helen. *She'll be a good cheerleader*, she thought.

"Let's try that one a couple of times," Lance's father said. "I want to make sure you have it down pat."

Helen did some of both flips. She knew she was doing them correctly, and she wasn't scared. She'd followed Lance's father's instructions.

"Let's take a five-minute break," Lance's mother said as she brought out the snacks and lemonade. Helen didn't want to eat anything but did have some lemonade.

"That's good thinking because I want you to try the flips without the safety belt," Lance's father said.

"You think I'm ready for that?" Helen asked.

"The question is whether you think you're ready for it."

Everyone looked at Helen. Dee winked at her and said, "I think she is."

Lance said, "I think so too."

Helen looked at her mother, who seemed worried. "What do you think, Mom?"

Her mother took a deep breath. Everyone was silent. "I'm so proud of what you're doing. I know if your father were here, he'd say go ahead. You go, girl!"

Everyone laughed

"Okay, I'm ready."

Everyone got around the trampoline to catch her if necessary. Lance's father even brought out some big cushions and put them in a circle behind everyone. "If you pass us, aim for the cushions," he said.

Helen nodded and began jumping, enjoying how the air felt. It wasn't as scary without the belt as she thought it would be.

Lance's father looked serious; he knew that if she didn't do it according to his instructions, she might hurt herself. All the spotters were concentrating on Helen's every move. She jumped higher and higher. When Lance's father yelled, "Tuck!" she executed a complete forward flip all by herself, landed correctly, and stopped perfectly. Helen couldn't believe she'd done it. *A miracle!*

Her mother was jumping. "My baby did it!" she kept saying. Dee was jumping, and Lance and Robert were giving each other high-fives.

"Man, did you see her? She was just like a professional gymnast," Robert said.

Lance was happy and proud at the same time. "I knew she could do it."

"What about a backflip?" Helen asked. Everyone was silent, and that scared Helen at first, but she said, "I'm ready to do it."

Lance's father called everyone around the trampoline. "Young lady, do exactly what I taught you."

Helen nodded and began jumping. Everyone quit breathing as Helen gained altitude. When she got to her highest point, Lance's father yelled, "Back!" The key word. She'd do a backflip on the next jump. She knew she was high enough. She went into the backflip and completed it. Everyone was amazed at her perfect posture. She landed right in the middle and stopped her bounce perfectly. Lance's father thought she'd be a good candidate to learn trampoline stunts. He was so proud of her.

He went up on the trampoline and started to jump with her. Lance, Dee, and Robert joined in the exciting moment. The women were in tears. Helen looked at them, and her mother said, "Happy tears! I'm so proud of what you've done!"

Helen looked at all the happy faces. "I couldn't have done this without you all around me. My street, my friends!"

She came down from the trampoline. "Thank you, Lance. I couldn't have done it without you. I hope we're friends forever." She kissed Lance on the lips, which left him speechless. His father winked, and his mother laughed and said, "For once someone has shut you up!"

Dee and Robert laughed. Lance thought, *I'm in love. She kissed me. On the lips!* It hadn't been a grown-up smooch, just a little smack, but it still put Lance on cloud nine.

Helen hugged Lance's father. "Thank you so much. You're a great teacher."

"I'm willing to teach you more if you want, but it'll have to wait till spring. Do you think you'll be able to do the loop to loop now?"

"No problem now! I'm ready for it. I'm not scared."

Everyone gathered around the snacks and ate everything in sight. Lance's mother went in for a second tray. *I knew they'd have an appetite when they got through.*

It was a happy Sunday for the neighbors. Everyone bragged about Helen, the superstar that day. The children went to Lance's garage to check out the extra details he had put on his scooter. "Man, where'd you get those great details?" Robert asked.

Lance told him an auto shop and said they could go there after school some time. Robert told him that would be great.

"We want to do girly stuff to ours!" Dee said.

They laughed and talked about the competition. They all felt they were good at what they did and were confident they'd be perfect. Helen told them she just wanted to do the loop to loop.

"Wait until coach sees this," Robert said. "He'll be so surprised."

They laughed again.

Dee's mother told her she wanted to go home and cook. Robert's father was ready to go, and Helen's mother was ready to go out and eat. They said their good-byes. The families had done something very special—they pulled together and supported Helen, who felt she was in a dream. She wished her father could have seen her.

She didn't know that Lance's mother had recorded the whole thing. She planned to upload it onto her computer and send it to Helen's mother so she could send it to Helen's father. *A moment like this need to be recorded,* she'd said to herself. *And it'll be a great gift for her father.*

She was proud Lance had suggested Helen learn the trampoline, and she was proud of her husband. *My man has a gift. He could teach children how to use the trampoline correctly.* She figured what she had recorded would be a great marketing tool if he wanted to make a business out of it.

Her husband was taking a shower. He felt great. *She did it. She's a great pupil, and I'm proud of her. What an accomplishment.* He got out of the shower and saw his wife looking at him admiringly.

"I was so proud about how you trained Helen. She looked like a pro!"

Lance's father smiled as she gave him a big hug and kiss. "I love you. Thanks for being my husband. Dinner will be ready in about hour."

Lance's father was too touched by what his wife had said to say anything. *She's a good egg. And I can just tell she's up to something.*

Lance was tired, but he helped his father take down the trampoline and store it. He showered and decided to be lazy for the rest of the day. He was about wash his face when he remembered the kiss Helen had given him in front of everyone. *Maybe she'll be my girlfriend when we get older.* He smiled. He'd enjoyed the day.

Helen and her mother had dinner at a buffet-style restaurant; Helen loved all-you-can-eat restaurants. Her mother was still looking at her with pride. "Helen, you're just like your father. He's not scared to do things either."

Helen smiled; she enjoyed hearing she was like her father. She knew her mother was a good person. She looked like her mother and felt she acted like her mother. "I'm glad you came over to help spot. Come on, tell me, were you scared?"

"To death! You're my only child, and I didn't want anything to happen to you, but I knew you had to do it. I was very proud of you. I love you very much, you know."

"Love you too, Mom."

They ate well; they both had good appetites even after the snacks at Lance's. "Let's do this again next Saturday after the competition," Helen said. "I don't think I'll win anything this year, but that's all right. I just want to do the loop to loop. You still working on my costume?"

"It's all done, and it looks very nice."

"When I get home, I'd like to try it on."

Dee, her mother, and her mother's friend walked home together feeling good about Helen. "Wasn't that great?" Dee asked.

"I've never seen anyone learn so fast. That girl is a natural," her mother said.

"I beg your pardon," Dee said, "but I can do much better. Don't you know?"

"I'm sorry. I was looking at it from Helen's point of view. I know you're good at it." She hugged Dee. "You're my daughter, and I'm so proud of you. You knew how to do that at age five, remember?"

Dee nodded. "Okay, you're forgiven."

They all laughed. Her mother's friend said, "How about we go over to my house? I have lasagna and a cake too. I need some assistance in eating it all."

Dee and her mother thought that was a good idea. They got into the friend's car and off they went.

Robert and his father were the first to leave. His father loved basketball, and the finals were on; his father never missed a game. Robert liked to watch too.

"How about that Helen?" his father asked on the way home. "Wasn't she good?"

"Yeah, and that was fun. But I was surprised you came. I thought you'd watch basketball all day."

"I know I don't spend the time I should with you, but I thought you were doing a good deed today, and I wanted to be a part of that. Besides, I wanted to be with you."

That surprised Robert. "You mean that, don't you?"

"Yes I do, son. I want to spend more time with my children, but at times, I have to make my work a priority. I have to pay our bills, put clothes on your backs, and buy food. You'll know what I'm talking about years from now. You have to try hard to take care of your family."

Robert nodded. "Thanks, Dad. You're all right!"

When his father rubbed his head, Robert realized that for once he didn't have his earphones on. *Whoa! But I really didn't miss it. I guess I was too busy spotting for Helen.*

His father started talking sports, but that was okay with Robert. He was listening. He was proud of his father. And he couldn't wait until he got home because he'd heard his mom was making sweet potato pie, and no one made that better.

"I bet I can beat you home!" his dad yelled as he sprinted off.

"You won't!"

Robert was surprised how fast his dad could run. He beat him to their yard, where they both lay in the grass on that beautiful day. The evenings were getting cooler. "Winter will be here soon, and you know what that means, right?" his father asked.

Robert rubbed his fingers together. "Yeah, Dad. Money!"

They laughed. Robert made more money in the winter shoveling for people than in any other season.

They went in and got ready to eat. Robert's sister was setting the table while his brother was watching basketball. Robert's father and Robert joined him.

"Dinner will be ready in fifteen minutes," Robert's mother said.

"We'll be cleaned up by then," Robert's father yelled.

"Momma, they didn't tell us how Helen did," said little sister.

"I know, baby," Robert's mother said. "You know boys can't miss their basketball. They'll tell us at dinner. We won't be able to shut them up."

They laughed as they prepared dinner.

When evening came, all the households were getting ready for the upcoming week. The children were finishing their homework. The mothers were making sure their lunches and clothes were ready. The fathers and Dee's mother were preparing to go to work in the morning. She thought, *I might have to work some overtime. I better see if Helen's mother can keep Dee.* She called Helen's mother. Helen answered. "Hi, Helen. Is your mother home?"

"Yes, I'll get her."

Dee's mother answered. Helen heard her mother say Dee could spend the night the next day, no problem. Helen was excited. *We can show each other our costumes!* She was glad her mother liked Dee and was friends with her mother. After

Helen's mother hung up, she let her know what the plan was, and Helen said she'd meet Dee after school.

The weekend had turned out okay. Everyone was looking forward to the competition on Saturday. The parents were excited because they knew how hard their children had worked. They would make sure they had enough fuel for their scooters; they'd made costumes and bought decorations for the scooters. They had paid for food and pop for the event, and some had volunteered to set up and clean up. It was a community project; the parents were just as involved as their children were.

The community center had been in the neighborhood since some of the parents were children; it had always been a place where everyone could meet. Kids could hang out there until their parents got home from work, and their parents couldn't live without it.

The coach thought it was the heartbeat of the neighborhood; he loved the place and was so excited about the competition he didn't know what to do with himself. He'd gone to the same church as Robert's family the previous Sunday and felt that same way Robert did. *That minister was dry.*

He got home and realized he didn't have anything for dinner, so he went out for some to-go. He lived a quiet life; he was thrilled when he was with children, who kept him young at heart. He drove to his favorite barbeque place and thought about all the kids who would compete. He worried about Dee. *She takes too many chances.*

He knew she was good, but he also knew she'd do things that made him shudder. She wasn't afraid of doing dangerous things, and he knew it was up to him to slow her down. He also worried about Helen, who wasn't confident enough to do the loop to loop. He wondered if he should tell her about not trying it. There was a simpler course for the younger children and beginners, but he knew that if he told her that, she'd get mad at him. He also knew he had to watch over them nonetheless; that was his responsibility. He was getting excited about it. He'd worked hard training them to do stunts, and some had turned out pretty good at that.

He turned down the street, saw Robert's open garage door, and spotted his shiny scooter. *Robert's been waxing it. Can't wait to see these kids do their thing Saturday. It's been a long time coming.* He drove on, feeling good about the competition. He felt it would be a good day and everyone would have fun. They were planning a picnic dinner afterward. He was hoping the weather would hold up. The weatherman on TV said about sixty-eight degrees, perfect for that time of year. He arrived at the restaurant hungry as could be and went in.

Chapter 8

The week had gone by so fast. The involved families had been preparing all week long. Lance had shown Robert, Dee, and Helen where he had gotten the detail for his scooter, an auto shop three blocks away. They'd gotten more decoration for their scooters and had been working hard to get them ready.

Dee's outfit colors matched her scooter's—pink and white with glitter. She'd gotten the glitter from the auto shop and thought it was a great addition to her scooter.

Helen's scooter was red and white while her outfit was black and red. She liked the combo. Her mother had made her outfit, which fit her perfectly. She'd made it out of stretchy material so she could move easily.

Lance's outfit, which his mother had made, was a colorful royal blue and gold. Lance was proud of it, as his scooter was royal blue.

Robert's scooter was black with silver trim. He'd made the neatest decorations on it, and it was cool. He had some tassels on the handlebars, and his outfit was all black, including his cool helmet, which he had ordered on the Internet. *Too cool!* he'd thought when he got it. His family had been shocked. "Robert, you look so strong and masculine!" his mother had said, and the rest of his family had remarked on how good he looked. Robert held his head up high. He was also proud of what he had accomplished. It would be a fun Saturday.

The time had come. It was Saturday. The competition was at one that afternoon, but the quartet had been up by eight. Their parents served them special breakfasts. Robert's father had gassed up his son's and Lance's scooters the night before and had checked out Dee's and Helen's to make sure theirs would run smoothly. *The least I can do for these girls. They don't have fathers to do that for them.*

The girls' mothers were grateful; it did make life easier for them. Dee and Helen were glad also; they were worried about their scooters. Dee remembered that her scooter hadn't started the previous week and that Robert had needed to help her. Robert's father volunteered to take the scooters to the community center while the mothers would bring the girls in their cars.

Time was ticking away. Everyone was getting nervous, especially Helen. Even though she had done those flips, she was nervous about doing the loop to loop. Lance had told her how to speed up right before she hit the loop. He told her it felt like the flips she did and just to let herself go and not worry about. *I hope he knows what he's talking about.* But she trusted Lance, her good friend. She was as ready as she would be. She got into her mother's car, and they took off.

Lance loaded his scooter onto a trailer bed, and his father made sure it was secure. "We can't have anything happening to this scooter now."

"That's right," said Lance. He was wound up about the competition. He had practiced so much and worked so hard on decorating his scooter. He had to concentrate, focus; no time to get scared, but he was a little anxious.

The obstacle course had been decorated and repainted. It looked wonderful. Bright-orange cones and flags marked off certain areas for stunts, as did the painted yellow and blue lines in the cement. Spectators could watch from some portable stands and form the cheering section. Parents had donated money for the food spectators could buy at the white-and-red food stand; the proceeds went to keeping the obstacle course up.

The coach came out with white jeans and a sharp, colorful jacket that said "Scooters." Everyone complimented him on how sharp he looked. He smiled and nodded. His thoughts were on the children. He had to double-check the scooters, make sure the judges knew what to look for, and check the children's safety equipment. It was fifteen minutes before the competition, so parents could run home and get the proper gear if necessary. He was a great coach.

The time had come. The coach told the twelve children to line up. The scooters were beautiful—so many colors and different designs, which the judges had to score along with the costumes and the stunts. It would be difficult; the children had worked hard.

The children were serious and quiet as they looked over the obstacle course. The coach told them how proud he was of them and to do their best. When he turned to the crowd and announced, "I'd like to introduce the competitors," everyone let out a loud cheer.

As each child's name was called, his or her family and friends cheered. "I wish I could give a trophy to the loudest cheer," the coach said, and everyone laughed.

The coach told the first child to get on his scooter. Everyone fell silent; the competitor needed to concentrate. He didn't do a perfect job; he missed a few things, but everyone clapped for him anyway. At least he had tried.

Lance was up next. Everyone loved how he looked and loved his scooter. He was a little nervous, but once he got started, he didn't even see the crowd. He handled the obstacle course and did all his stunts perfectly, prompting the crowd to roar. His father and mother jumped up and down in the stands; they were so proud. They ran over to congratulate him. *That was his greatest performance yet!* his father thought.

Other children did their stunts. Some of them did just the basics but did them well. No one had fallen. The parents and friends were yelling their lungs out each time a child completed his or her stunts. The weather was perfect—blue skies, puffy white clouds, and no breeze. He was proud of the children, the parents, and the neighborhood. All of them had volunteered and worked hard. *This is a great success.*

Dee was up next. The coach held his breath because he knew Dee would try something new. *Lord, please protect this child.*

Dee was awesome; she did stunts no one else could, and she had a new move. All eyes were on her as she stood on the seat while the scooter was moving. She made it back down, and she did her famous trick of holding her legs up high backward while holding onto the handlebars. She completed her stunts perfectly. Everyone stood up and gave her a standing ovation.

Her mother was jumping up and down. She couldn't believe Dee had done that amazing trick. She ran down to give her a hug. When Dee realized she had done all her tricks well, she jumped up and down.

This will be hard for me to beat, Robert thought just when Old Man Davis came over. "You know you're good, boy. I know you can do this." The old man walked away while looking back at Robert.

Robert's family was sitting on the edge of their seats. When they called his name, his mother grabbed her heart and held her breath. She was always worried about him doing his stunts.

Robert got on the scooter. The coach gave him the signal to go. Robert revved up his engine and took off. He went through the basic course expertly. *That was easy.* He was in his zone, concentrating on what he was doing. He did some tricks he'd practiced many times. He stood on the seat of the scooter and held his legs in a handstand, and the crowd applauded. He did all his tricks perfectly, including jumping off the scooter while it was going, running alongside, and then jumping back on. The crowd stood up and screamed. Robert had done it. He was as talented as Dee. His father couldn't contain himself. Old Man Davis was also doing his best to jump up and down, but his feet never left the cement. He waved and yelled, "Bravo, Robert, bravo!" *I must go to the bank Monday and do what I've wanted to do for a long time— open a college trust fund for Robert.* He smiled as he thought how excited Robert's family would be.

Next up was the Somalian girl, who had practiced so hard. Though her father was against it, he was there along with her mother, siblings, and family friends. Her father had allowed her to wear jeans, and she had a scarf around her hair under her helmet.

She revved her engine. She was confident she could do the basics, and she did. Then to everyone's surprise she did the loop to loop. The coach's eyes widened. *Never underestimate the power of a woman.* He smiled, and she received a standing ovation.

Her father couldn't believe his daughter was so brave. He ran to her and gave her a huge hug as her family cheered her. Her father looked at the coach, touched his heart, and bowed. That was the most rewarding moment in the coach's career, and everyone else was touched by this token of gratitude. Tears were in the father's eyes. They'd experienced so much hardship back in their country; they knew they had picked the right community to live in.

Two other children were before Helen. She was a little worried. She felt a little pain in her stomach. She tried to fight it, but it wouldn't go away. *If my father were here, he'd tell me to do my best no matter what. He told me, "Life is to be lived, so whatever you do, have fun doing it."* Remembering his words gave her confidence; the pain in her stomach went away. She took a few deep breaths and pulled her scooter to the starting line. Lance came up to her and whispered, "Remember what we taught you Sunday. When you get to the loop to loop, speed up and just go. It'll feel like a flip on the trampoline. The coach is going to be real surprised." He smiled and kissed her cheek.

She was surprised at that, but she liked it and smiled. "I'll be all right."

The coach checked her equipment. "You know you don't have to do the loop to loop if you don't want to. Just do what you're confident about, okay?"

"Don't worry coach. I'm okay. Watch me." She revved her engine.

Her mother, even though she was worried, smiled at her daughter and nodded that it was okay to do it.

Helen felt great; she did all the basics perfectly. She took the course to the loop to loop.

What's that girl doing? the coach thought. He wanted to stop her, but it was too late.

Helen headed for the loop to loop. All her friends were holding their breaths. *Remember the flip*, Helen repeated to herself. She came to the last straightaway before the loop to loop and sped up. Before she knew it, she was in the loop to loop. She was surprised that it did feel like the flips she'd done on the trampoline. She'd done it. Her mother was crying tears of joy. Helen was so happy that she held her legs out on the sides when she came to a stop. She got off the scooter and jumped up and down. Her mother ran down the stands to hug her daughter. Everyone was surrounding Helen like she was a super star. *I guess I am a star today. I actually did it!* She was getting a little teary eyed herself.

The coach was surprised. *That girl actually did it.* He made his way through the people and gave her a big hug. "I knew you'd someday tackle that old loop to loop. I just didn't know it was today!"

"Thanks coach," she said. "You're the greatest coach I've ever had." Just when she was getting ready to go back to her scooter, she heard a familiar voice.

"I'm so proud of you, Helen. Come here!"

Helen couldn't believe her eyes. It was her father. She let go of her scooter and ran right into his arms; she wrapped her legs around her father.

Her mother couldn't believe her eyes either. "Oh My God!" she yelled and ran as fast as she could. Their eyes met as he was hugging Helen. Everyone gave the loudest applause ever. Her tall, handsome father was in his uniform with medals on his chest.

The neighbors ran down to greet Helen's father. Helen's mother asked him, "How did you manage to get here?"

"I've been wounded!"

Helen slowly let go of her father. She felt she might hurt him. Her mother started to cry.

"Honey, don't do that. I'm alive!" He gave her a big kiss and hug. "Let's sit and finish watching the competition. This is the best medicine I could have. What a homecoming for me!"

Helen, her mother, and her father walked hand in hand to stands. Her father was limping badly. "Your leg, Daddy?"

He nodded. "I got shot in the knees, baby, but I'll be okay, and with you all around me, I know I'll heal fast." He looked at his wife, who was worried. "Honey, I'll heal up and continue working, but I won't go back to the war."

He seemed sad when he said that, but Helen thought he should be happy about that.

Old Man Davis stood at attention and gave her dad a salute, which her dad returned. It was a touching moment that had most of the crowd in tears.

"I'm glad to be back home today," he yelled to everyone.

They all stood and gave him a standing ovation. Helen and her mother couldn't let go of him father as they watched the rest of the competition. *This is way better than even Christmas!* thought Helen. *And wait till he sees the garden. He'll be surprised!* Helen was proud of how hard she had worked to keep their garden up while her dad was gone. Once he healed up, she knew he would be back tending the garden. She thought she would need to continue working it until he healed up.

Helen's friends surrounded her. Robert said, "Man, you should have seen yourself. I think Lance's mother taped it. We're going to watch it and have some popcorn too!" They laughed and hugged each other.

"That sounds fun!"

"I'm glad your father's home," Robert said. "Our dads will be watching the basketball games, so get ready."

They laughed.

Dee was happy for Helen but a little sad about herself. *Everyone has a father but me.*

Her mother must have known what she was thinking. She hugged her. "It'll be all right, honey. If you think about it, you have family all around you."

Dee had never thought of it that way. Her mother was right. Everyone on her street was part of her life. They all helped each other. There had been many times when her friend's fathers would come to the house and fix things. Her street was a good neighborhood. Her friends were good friends. *I really don't need to worry about it. I'm okay.*

After hugging her mother back, Dee locked up her scooter and sat with her friends. She thought about the good times she'd had with her mother and her mother's best friend. *I'll be all right. There's no need for me to be sad. I have many fathers on my street.*

The crowd watched the rest of children complete their stunts. Everyone completed the obstacle course with no accidents. Everyone patted the coach's back and thanked him. The coach looked tired. He worried about each child and did his best to make sure they were safe while they were competing. He had done an excellent job.

It was time for the judging. Everyone was sitting on the edge of the seats. The judges were having a difficult time because all the children had done well. They were huddled in discussion. The crowd was ready to celebrate and eat. Finally, the judges stood. One yelled, "We have made our decision." Everyone was as quiet as could be. "First place goes to Dee!"

The crowd stood and cheered. Dee couldn't believe it. Her mother had to coax her to get up and receive her award—$1,000 to go into a trust fund for college. Dee kissed and hugged her mother and ran to the judges for her trophy and the statement of money. She couldn't get the money until she graduated from high school, but that was all right. She had won.

"Robert wins second place!"

That meant $500 toward his college education. His family was excited. They hugged him as he got up to receive his trophy. He didn't mind winning second; he knew Dee had worked hard, and her stunts were way over his head. He was proud of himself and was glad his family was too. "Hey bro! You won!" his brother yelled and gave him a high-five. "You'll probably win another scholarship next year," he said.

"Yeah, if I can beat Dee. She needs to show me how she makes those moves."

"Yeah, right, like she's going to show you!"

Robert's dad was teary eyed. "You're just a big, old teddy bear," his wife said.

He hugged her. "I'm proud of my whole family!"

"Hey Dad, I want a scooter!" Robert's sister said.

Her father looked at her. "Oh Lord, here we go again!" They all laughed.

Old Man Davis had overheard their conversation. *They have more surprises to come.* Monday morning, I am going to add to that college account. *That boy will make it someday, and I might as well help him. I don't want them thinking they have to do anything for me. I just want to help Robert because he does so much for me around the house. He's a good boy.*

Some of the retired women were preparing food at the picnic area. They loved to do things for the community. The coach had gotten his favorite barbeque restaurant to cater the picnic. *I like those older women, but they can't cook well*, he thought.

The caterer's van arrived with chicken, ribs, and hot dogs ready to go. The women scurried to get the trays onto the tables. Some of them had made potato salad and desserts. Some of the community staffers were covering the picnic tables, blowing up balloons, and putting up other decorations. The DJ was setting up. What's a picnic without music? And this would be a good picnic. After the judges were finished announcing the awards, everyone would be hungry.

The judges announced the third place winner. To everyone surprise, it was Helen, who didn't realize for a couple of seconds that she had won. Her father said, "Don't you want to get your trophy?"

Helen looked at her friends jumping up and down. "Yeah!" She ran to get her trophy and award, $100 for college education. Her father was home, and she had won. *This is the best day ever!*

Helen's mother was overcome; her husband hugged her. "I got my man back, and my daughter won third place. Nothing could be better than this!"

Helen showed her trophy to her parents. She didn't want him to walk too much because she knew his knees hurt; she could tell by the way he was limping. *I'll take care of my daddy.*

Lance and his family were surprised that he hadn't won, but Lance didn't mind; he was glad Helen had won. She'd worked very hard. He was glad it was over. He determined to practice more and worry about his costume and scooter decorations less. He was hungry.

His father was surprised about how he was taking it. "I'm proud of you, son. You're becoming a man right in front of my eyes." He gave his son a big hug.

Lance's mother was filming everything; that was one of her hobbies. *I might try to publish this. It's great stuff.* She was always thinking about ways to make money, and she felt what she had gotten on tape was worth the effort. She joined her family and friends as they went to the picnic area. The food smelled wonderful, even the grilled vegetables for those who didn't eat meat. There was plenty for everyone.

Kids were playing in the grass, and the adults chatted and gossiped as they ate. One older woman was flirting with Old

Man Davis, who was doing his best to escape. Robert laughed and told his friends about it.

"You stop laughing at him," the coach said, but he was in tears himself from laughing so hard himself. "Look at that old man go!"

Of course, Old Man Davis didn't think it was particularly funny. "Leave me alone, girl!" he hollered.

The DJ started the music with some hip-hop. He had a mix of all kinds of music, but since it was the kids' day, he started off with a bang. The kids ran to the dance area as did some of the adults. The party was on.

Robert, Lance, Helen, and Dee started dancing to their hearts' content.

Two songs later, when the DJ announced, "Time for the electric slide!" everyone headed to the dance floor, even those who didn't know what the electric slide was. About a hundred people, adults and children, were dancing away and having fun, celebrating the competition, and enjoying the company.

The coach watched children playing some games and winning awards donated by some of the local businesses. *This is what it's all about. I'm blessed to be here. The children are so good, and they all worked so hard. Bless those older women for laying out all the food. And look at all the different cultures out there doing the electric slide!*

He loved the children and his community. He knew it was a strong one, and the kids needed that center. Each year, they would ask for a grant to continue services and raise money by holding different functions. He hoped it would continue forever.

Chapter 9

The picnic ended by eight that evening. Everyone was tired and full. Many parents had assisted in cleaning up, and Robert and Lance did too. The older women were too tired to clean; they were sitting and fanning themselves. Old Man Davis had finally outrun his pursuer. *That lady's crazy if she thinks I want to get married again.* But he had to chuckle at himself. *I still got it, though.*

Lance, Helen, Dee, and Robert were tired. Robert's father went to get his pickup to take the scooters home. "You all were great today," he said. "You made your parents proud."

They were still beaming. They had worked hard to get to this point.

"Mom, Helen asked me to spend the night today. Can I?" Dee asked her mother.

That was okay with her mom, who wanted to go to a movie with her best friend. "Did Helen's mother say it was okay? Her daddy just got home."

Helen's mother came up. "It's okay. Tonight will be a movie night for them. I'll make popcorn."

"Thank you, especially since your husband just got home."

"Don't worry," Helen's mother said. "He's going to bed early. He's tired and in pain. I'll be the nurse for a while now. Helen will need company while I tend to him."

Dee's mother hugged Helen's mother. Dee got into her mother's car and waved at Helen. "See you later!" she yelled.

Lance's father had gotten his scooter into the trailer. Lance told Helen, "Hey, I'm going to ask my parents if I can go to the movies. Do you think you and the others will be able to go?"

"I'm going to stick around the house and help my mother take care of my daddy," Helen said. "He's in a lot of pain and needs our help."

"I'd forgotten about that," Lance said. "I'll see you sometime tomorrow. How about if we ride our bikes now that the scooter thing's over?"

"Yeah! Let's ride around tomorrow. Dee's spending the night. I'll ask her if she wants to go too."

"And I'll ask Robert if he wants to go," Lance said.

"And we can get ice cream cones!" Helen said, licking her lips. She loved her friends. She couldn't imagine another place like her street.

"See you tomorrow afternoon," Robert said. He ran home thinking about Helen. *She'll be my girlfriend!* He saw Robert. "You want to go bike riding tomorrow afternoon with us?"

"I got to finished cleaning out Old Man Davis's garage," Robert said. "I should be finished about two."

"Meet us at the ice cream shop."

Robert nodded and ran home to take a shower.

"Robert," his father said, "I'm proud of you!"

That surprised Robert. "Thanks, Dad. I'm proud to have you as my father. You're always there for me. I used to get mad at you when you were never home, but now I know why. You have to work hard to pay the bills for the family. And we got a big family, don't we?"

They laughed, knowing Robert was right.

"Go take your shower. Your mother baked a chocolate fudge cake, and I bought vanilla ice cream."

"Now that's what I'm talking about!" yelled Robert, who ran upstairs to take a shower. *I'll never forget this day.* He was sad he had to put up his scooter, but he knew the rules; scooters couldn't be rode on the streets after the competition as a safety precaution. The adults had to make sure that the fuel was emptied and properly disposed of. Most of their scooters were stored in their parents' garages. *That's okay. I need to dust my bike off and put some air in the tires. My friends and I can talk about the competition tomorrow.*

Sunday morning came around. Robert's alarm woke him up at nine. He had a hard time getting up, but he wanted to finish cleaning out Old Man Davis's garage. He got up slowly. The house was quiet. He put on his work clothes, went downstairs, and made some cereal. He was wishing he didn't have to work that day, but he had promised Mr. Davis. He put his bowl in the sink and headed out.

Mr. Davis was on his front porch waiting for Robert and drinking coffee. "Good morning, Robert. I didn't think you'd come."

"It was hard getting up this morning. I'm tired from yesterday, but I slept well. I'm ready to finish the garage."

"Good of you. You'll find equipment in the garage."

Robert got to work as Mr. Davis read his newspaper. He shivered in the chill. *Winter's coming. I'm glad I have Robert to shovel snow.*

Dee had slept well in the guest bedroom at Helen's house. She woke up and smelled something good being prepared for breakfast. She took a shower while Helen was still sleeping. Her father was still sleeping too, but her mother was up making breakfast.

Her mother was so happy to have her husband back. She'd been waiting so long for him. She was determined to nurse him back to health and then go on a vacation. She knew Helen would help with the chores. She was making her husband's favorite breakfast, pancakes and sausage. *I'll make ten just for him, and I'll take them up to him. I know he won't eat all of them, but Dee will finish them up.* She always likes Dee. She was a bit strong willed, but a good girl, and she never minded having her over. She and Helen were like sisters

Dee came downstairs. "I could smell breakfast cooking. It woke me up."

"You can help me, Dee. In five minutes, we'll wake up. You two can eat here while I visit with my husband."

Dee nodded and started to help.

Meanwhile, Helen was having a good dream about the previous day. When she woke up, she wondered, *Was that just a dream, or did my dad really come home?* She almost panicked when she heard someone come into her room.

"Hey there," her father said.

Helen jumped out of bed and hugged him, being very careful not to bump his knees. "I'm so glad you're home! Go back to bed! I'll help momma today."

"You're so grown up, young lady. I noticed the garden and was so surprised. Your mother told me how hard you worked on it. Thank you!"

"You're welcome, Daddy. I'm just glad you're home."

They hugged, and Helen went to take a shower. She could smell the breakfast also. *Pancakes!* She put on her jogging outfit and ran downstairs. Her mother had her plate ready. "Momma, Daddy's awake!"

"Okay. I'll bring breakfast to him. You two be good and eat your breakfast. I'm sure I don't have to worry!"

She had a very energetic step as she left the kitchen. Dee had already begun her breakfast. "You beat me, didn't you?" Helen asked. Dee just smiled and ate.

Lance was still sleeping when he father came into his room. His father had stayed home from church. "There's no need to go today," he'd told his wife. "He needs his rest, and I don't think the reverend will mind if we don't come."

His wife nodded. She didn't want to go to church either. "I'm going to run to the store right quick," he said. "You need anything?"

She shook her head. Lance's father left; she went into the living room and stretched out on the sofa. She was very tired from the day before. She was so proud of her neighborhood and how everyone had pitched in. She was glad she had documented the whole affair. *I'll edit this film and show it at the community center.* She was trying to think of a name for it. *Maybe I'll call it what I heard Helen say when she was thanking us for teaching her to do her flips. I was so proud of her. Maybe I'll call it, "My Street, My Friends." That has a nice ring to it.*

Helen's such a nice girl, and I think my son has a crush on her. She chuckled at the thought. She dozed off on the couch.

The day had gone well for everyone in the neighborhood. Robert finished Old Man Davis's garage and was surprised when he gave him $50 for his work. He hadn't been expecting that much. He ran home to show his parents, and they were surprised too. "I'll put twenty-five in the bank and treat myself with the rest!"

His parents laughed. They were proud of him, knowing they had raised him right.

Later that day, the children met up at Dee's house to ride their bikes to the coffee shop. They knew the days were getting shorter. They donned their helmets and mounted their bikes. The day was beautiful. The streets were covered in leaves. The squirrels were looking for nuts. The children were laughing and talking about the competition. This time, you didn't hear the loud humming of the scooters. They were stored away till next year.

Printed in the United States
By Bookmasters